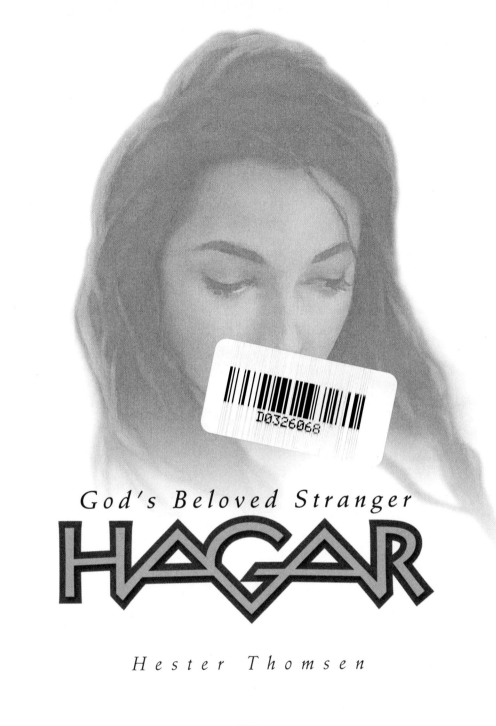

God's Beloved Stranger

HAGAR

Hester Thomsen

REVIEW AND HERALD® PUBLISHING ASSOCIATION
HAGERSTOWN, MD 21740

The author assumes full responsibility for the accuracy of all facts
and quotations as cited in this book.

This book was
Edited by Gerald Wheeler
Designed by Trent Truman
Cover Illustration by Todd Leonardo
Electronic makeup by Shirley M. Bolivar
Typeset: Stemple Schneidler 11/14

PRINTED IN U.S.A.

07 06 05 04 03   5 4 3 2 1

R&H Cataloging Service
Thomsen, Hester, 1914-2001
        Hagar: God's beloved stranger

        I. Title.

ISBN 0-8280-1632-1

Contents

Introduction

This book is the culmination of 25 years of research. I gleaned insights from anthropology, archaeology, history, ancient legends, and the Bible as well as from six years of archaeological field experience in Palestine. As I've attempted to recapture Hagar's emotions and the world in which she lived, I've had to reconstruct the social, religious, and political issues of her lifetime. Hagar's first home was in Egypt during the twelfth dynasty (1990-1785 B.C.). An odd combination of logic, magic, and mysticism dominated her world. The ruling Egyptians focused on preserving their names and bodies for eternity.

Opulent though this environment was, young Hagar chose to leave it to cast her lot with Abraham's people, the "Sand-dwellers" of Canaan. Abraham lived under Amorite city-kings during the Middle Bronze Period. Many villages dotted the landscape. During the Twelfth Dynasty, Egyptian pharaohs built and manned a series of forts along the Canaan coast to protect their trade routes.

The climate in Palestine was distinctly different from that of Egypt. During most years the rain would bring to life the green pastures in the plains, hills, and valleys that the shepherds roamed. But at times the land suffered severe drought.

For the central characters I used actual biblical and historical figures but invented a few minor ones to fill out the story. The dialogue often employs actual phrases translated from Egyptian writings and inscriptions of the time. Their written sentences were short, picturesque, and full of personifications of both ideas and objects. For example, the ancient near east regarded the heart as equivalent to what we would call the mind. Far more than just a symbol for the emotions, people considered the heart the actual center of reason and all thinking.

Hagar was born and grew up in the royal household. Sometimes the Egyptian terms for it *(ipit, per-khener)* are translated as harem, but that confuses it with the Turkish harem, which was quite different from the Egyptian one. The Egyptian harem was the royal palace in which the royal women lived and produced many goods (such as woven linen) for the Egyptian economy. To avoid the misleading connotation of harem, this book refers to the institution either as the household of the women or royal household.

The Heir

A cry mingled with far-off voices jerked Hagar awake. Her heart throbbing, she sat upright. The fumes from the burning oil lamps hung heavy in the air and their flickering flames stirred the shadows. Through the open door of her goat-hair tent she saw the moon above the wind-driven oak trees "Like Sinuhe," she whispered, "I've chosen to tent with the Sand-dwellers, to become one of them. But yesterday I flaunted a custom of their land. Now what?"

A fretful wail fully awakened her. Still weak from childbirth she knelt on a sheepskin to lift her son for his night feeding. The delicate hollows in her olive cheeks filled with tears and she swayed as she chanted a lullaby from her Egyptian homeland:

"Hast thou come to kiss this child?
I will not let thee kiss him!
Hast thou come to silence him?
I will not let thee set silence over him!
Hast thou come to injure him?
I will not let thee injure him!
Hast thou come to take him away?
I will not let thee take him from me!"

As she sang her wide-set, dark eyes glanced over her shoulder toward the entrance. Then she ended the song softly lest she wake the infant in her arms. After laying him on his bed of sheepskins she leaned back on her heels and told herself, "I will not think about this. I must not think about it." As she hugged the child against her, her thoughts shouted with each beat of her heart, *You are mine! I will take care of you! I will fight for you.* At that moment a decision formed, one that had been growing for many days and nights. *I will be the favored wife. You shall be heir and father of kings.*

Brushing away the remaining tears, she returned to her bed. Unfortunately, sleep eluded her. The night was cool but she knew the blazing sun would soon bring another hot day.

Hagar watched the moonlight filter through the oaks into her tent. In the distance the black tents of the shepherds silhouetted themselves against the backdrop of motionless hills. Nothing but the eerie call of owls broke the stillness. "Who else is awake?" she asked herself. "Is the father of my son?"

The question released a wave of bitterness. "My eyes are fountains of tears," she wailed in the idioms of her people. "My feet sink in quicksand. It is unreal." A deep shuddering breath escaped her.

When she grew a little calmer memories began to slip silently into her thoughts. Her heart unrolled the papyrus of her early years in Pharaoh's household.

In the Land of the Nile

"You're Pharaoh's lowest daughter!"

"You're nothing but the child of a bondwoman."

"Whatever can we possibly do with you?"

"Why is the floor covered with water?"

"Keep the truth and don't exceed it!"

"Hagar, speak when we address you."

"Don't answer with silence!"

The accusations and questions slashed at Hagar's heart and the angry looks from the older women threatened to tear her apart. As other servants rushed in to deal with the problem, Hagar lifted her long linen skirt and fled. She pretended not to hear Maraket, the royal household overseer, call after her. Uncontrolled tears blinded her as she stumbled to her refuge in the garden.

Once safely behind the oleanders, she yanked the red flowers from the lancelike leaves, tore them into ribbons, and flung the shreds to the ground. Through clenched teeth she raged, "They don't love me. It's not fair. It's really not fair.

"Why am I trapped in a household of powerful women who care nothing about me? I wish I were in my mother's tomb embalmed for eternity. I need a mother to intercede for me in Pharaoh's palace."

At that moment she resented the women of the royal household. At times they treated her as a daughter, other times as nothing more than a servant. She ran errands, cared for infants, and watched the younger children—some of them her half brothers and sisters. The royal wives had no legal claim upon Pharaoh for either themselves or their children, yet she yearned for him to notice her as his daughter.

The happy voices of children entering the garden jostled Hagar's emotions. "They've already forgotten the mess," she sighed. Her love for them momentarily chased her problems into the shadows of her heart for the royal children were her family.

One small girl held a cat while others carried painted wooden dolls. Older girls, wearing white linen dresses and braided hair, juggled balls and played catch. Groups of boys with their heads shaved except for a braided Egyptian sidelock played "going round four times." One boy held a stick and enticed a dog to jump over it. Others floated toy boats on the lotus pool. In the sand in a far corner small hands shaped rows of pyramids and palaces. "At least children accept me," she reminded herself. "I'll sit and watch them."

She admired the orderliness, symmetry, and form of the garden. A high blue and white wall set it apart from the palace and the rest of Egypt. Into it the outside world hardly penetrated, making her feel confined instead of protected.

Hagar glanced at the garden's focal point, a mirror-like lotus pool stocked with fish. The white and rose-purple lotus flowers floated on flat leaves spread out on the water. Artfully spaced clumps of flowers and shrubs surrounded the pool. The blue cornflowers resembled fragments of the sky, and the hot sun intensified the sweet fragrance of jasmine.

Many times, during the mysterious moments between sunset and dark, she'd come to this garden to dream of being free to make her own choices. During such free moments there she felt a great longing for things that she did not quite know or understand. Often she wondered what lay beyond the horizon punctuated by the date and dom palms. Through the screen of sycamore figs she glimpsed the extensive orchards, vineyards, and onion and melon fields of her native land.

As she watched, Baufra, the gardener, and his grandson, Khuni, emerged from the orchard. Baufra supervised the gardeners who kept the immediate surroundings in parklike condition. He was more like a father to her than Pharaoh. Many times his counsel would set the world right again. When the two came nearer she carefully placed her bare feet on the hot earth and went to meet them, calling, "Baufra, Baufra, Khuni, I need your ears."

Baufra looked at her closely and teased, "You honor us by asking for our ears."

"I must speak of secret things. The household women fill my heart with heaviness."

His eyes twinkled. "Dare you again let me, an old man, know the secrets of the royal household?"

"But Baufra . . ."

"Hagar, don't you know that scribes write royal household secrets with wind in running water?"

"But Baufra, all my happiness has vanished. Pharaoh's wives have cast goodness to the ground. Their mouths sprout evil. They slander and accuse me of things I haven't done"

The old man searched Hagar's face. "What is this, a whole bag of little things? Does your heart enlarge your problems? Are they really as bad as you think?"

"Wait, I'll tell you. Earlier today a donkey caravan stopped at the gate. Maraket took all the women and maidservants to buy cosmetics, leaving nearly 100 children in my care."

He stooped to pick some faded blossoms. "Good, you love children, so your heart filled with gladness?"

She shook her head. "No. Joy fled my heart. The children played Egyptians at war with Nubians. They threw water, tracked in sand, and left mud. They hurled fruit and bread at their enemies, in the process knocking over stools and chairs."

"What did you do?"

"What could I do when they ignored me? Then their mothers returned."

"And the game came to an abrupt halt," Khuni finished.

She nodded. "And they blamed everything on me. When I tried to explain they wouldn't listen. I don't know how to please them. I need a heart skilled in hardship. What can I do?" Hagar demanded.

The gardener shook his head. "Hagar, you can learn much from such trials. Just try a little harder to please them. Choose to obey all that is asked. Don't be arrogant toward them. Remember, gone is that which yesterday saw. This too will pass."

"Baufra, you always speak well. My heart chooses to follow the counsel from your heart."

"Hagar, remember the sky is serene after a storm." He bent to pull a small weed at his feet.

"Not in the household of the royal women. There's always a storm going on. Each of the women try to be first in Pharaoh's eyes. They grab favors from the palace for their children. Then jealousy and anger flares when some receive favors and others don't."

"When Pharaoh and his army return from Nubia, the household will grow quiet again." Baufra turned to Khuni, "Today the gardeners are using the shaduf to water the orchards. But the chrysanthemums are dry. Khuni, you and Hagar soak each plant with water from the lotus pool."

As a small child Hagar had tagged after Baufra offering her help. A wise teacher, he taught her the proper care of each plant and tree. From him she had learned the names of her land's trees, shrubs, flowers, and weeds. As she grew older she found that the work distracted her from her worries. Maybe it would make today's problem disappear for a while.

A breeze shimmered the reflections of Hagar and Khuni on the surface of the pool as water gurgled into their jars. Fish darted to investigate the disturbance while frogs slithered under the lotus pads.

"Khuni, do you want to go to Nubia or to the land of the Sand-dwellers when you serve in Pharaoh's army?"

He handed her another jar of water. "I won't join Pharaoh's army."

"Why not? Pharaoh's sons are officers. He'd make you one too."

Khuni stood. "Someday I'll be a merchant with donkey caravans and cargo boats. They'll go to Lebanon and Nubia."

"But why not the army?" she persisted.

"Because I want to work with donkeys and with boats. And travel. Father says it is good to be a merchant."

Hagar poured water around a thirsty plant. "If only I were a boy," she sighed. "When Pharaoh comes home he'll take the 12-year-old boys in the household of the women to live in the royal palace. He will train them as officers in the army. I'm 14. Pharaoh will find me a husband. I hope he isn't a priest."

"You want to marry a soldier?"

"No, a merchant. Like Pharaoh and you, I would like to travel to far away places."

"I'm going to travel," Khuni said. "I'm 18. When I'm an important merchant, maybe Pharaoh will give me a wife." His jar slipped to the bottom of the pool and he struggled to pull it to the surface.

"When are you going to be a merchant?"

"As soon as I can find someone who will take me on."

Hagar remained silent. She didn't want to marry a priest or a soldier. Could she forestall Pharaoh finding a husband for her until Khuni became a great merchant? Would the women in the household help her?

"We must wait," Khuni whispered. "We must wait."

Hagar and Khuni had no way of knowing that a drought had swept over a distant country and that a stranger from there was already in the Two Lands and would alter both their futures.

The girl stared at something in the distance. "Khuni, I see a messenger from the palace. I must find out what is going on. Take my jar."

Pharaoh's Return

Out of breath, Hagar reached the women's quarters in time to hear the messenger announce that "Pharaoh rests at 'Mighty-is-Khekure.' If the north winds are quiet at the first cataract he'll be here in five days. Have everything ready." Hagar's father would soon be home. A sense of excitement swept over her.

The household of the women sprang into action as commands from Pharaoh's wives resounded from room to room. Servants scrubbed floors, removed spider webs and sand and dust, and washed linen dresses. Special foods arrived from the markets. Kitchen servants prepared special dishes that could survive for several days in the hot dry air. Each day the great piles of sesame seed cakes grew taller. Hagar's mouth watered. Pharaoh would not eat with them, but the women's palace would feast while he banqueted in his own palace.

Tasnek, one of Pharaoh's most scheming wives, paused when she saw Hagar. "I need you. Go with my maid Nakht to the palace. They require help in the brewery. Stay with her and return when she's finished. Try to hear everything and report to me."

Luck just fell on me, Hagar thought to herself. *When I return the other women will listen to me. My heart leaps for joy.*

Activity seemed even more feverish in the palace. Going down a wide hall they saw an arched opening leading to a spacious room. Scribes sat cross-legged on the floor, which stretched the front of their white linen kilts tight and provided a desk for the papyrus paper. The scribes wrote from right to left with their reed brushes. Wishing that girls could be scribes in the house of learning, Hagar longed to read the fine hieratic writing.

The scribes seemed unaware of them so the girls crept to the doorway to hear better as the palace bureaucrats discussed recent events among themselves. One scribe spoke of a great merchant prince who had come to the Two-Lands. "Abram stands high among the chiefs in Palestine," he said. "Because his land has had drought for a long time, he brought his people here until the rains return. He's a wealthy trader with large donkey caravans."

Another scribe paused, holding up his writing brush, "I hear he wishes to establish trade contacts in our land." He thought a moment. "The strangest thing is that he and his people carry no gods with them. Instead they worship a god they can't see."

A short scribe stood, stretching his legs. "Abram is a man of unusual wisdom and impressive knowledge. He teaches with great power. Many of our people flock to him to hear about his God."

A third scribe, sitting close to the door, added, "They say Abram has a sister of exceptional beauty."

Someone laughed, then added, "Pharaoh is sure to add her to his household. A messenger has already notified Pharaoh of their presence." When Hagar made a sound, a scribe glanced in their direction and motioned the girls away.

They walked past the huge stores of grain to the bakery. The sour, yeasty odor in the next room warned the girls that brewing was in progress. Inside a servant carried barley to a man who cracked it in a mortar. Nakht was assigned to grind it into coarse flour on a limestone mill, a task reserved for women.

Hagar saw a man take the coarse flour from the catch basin, add water and a yeasty dough, then form his mixture into loaves. He set the loaves on a low stove to rise and partially bake. Then another man crumbled them into basins of water and stepped in to tread the mass with his feet. It would ferment until a thick lumpy liquid formed. After sieving it they would store it in jars for Pharaoh's welcome feast.

Hagar gleaned all the gossip she could about Abram's sister and the royal wife, Nefershent.

When they returned to the household of the women, Tasnek's maid went to share her news with other servants while Hagar repeated what she had heard to the royal wives and daughters. Their eager attention made her feel important. "The great chieftain's sister is the most beautiful of all women. They say she is very fair. She may come to live here." Hagar noticed Tasnek's body tense. The woman's powerful influence made everyone careful what they said in her presence. Her enemies had a habit of suddenly disappearing. Gossip had it they were thrown in the Nile to be eaten by crocodiles and thus destroyed for eternity.

"She won't lord it over us," Tasnek said quietly.

"But if she's so fair, she will be Pharaoh's favorite," another predicted.

"Let's hope she's beautiful with a heart full of feathers, slow and stupid," one of the younger women suggested.

"Jealousy burns like fire," another reminded, laughing. With that they all went back to their tasks.

Servants running errands between the palace and the household of the women brought additional bits of gossip. No more news however came about the great chieftain and his sister.

Guest
at the Palace

{ornamental border}

On the fourth day after Pharaoh's return Meraket's servant gave Hagar a message. She went at once to the overseer. Kheti and other girls followed.

When Meraket saw the girls, he said, "The palace sends orders for you to dance and sing at a banquet in honor of Abram the merchant prince. He is Sen Wosret's guest. Go to the palace as soon as Amon Re rides high in the sky. Meru will meet you there."

"Our ears will listen," Kheti whispered to Hagar. "We should pick up a lot of gossip. It will definitely not be a dull day."

"The palace scribes say Abram is a Sand-dweller of great wisdom," Hagar replied.

When the girls arrived at the palace, Hagar swept the banquet room with a quick glance. The court chamberlains, priests, scribes, and minor princes gathered in clusters. The king's spies and guards milled through the crowd. Close to His Majesty sat Sebek-Khu, military commander assigned to deal with the Sand-dwellers. Another man, his short well-trimmed beard of the deepest black, listened closely to Pharaoh. About three hands taller than the Egyptians, he had a determined business-like look. His smile seemed to come from his eyes as well as his mouth. Hagar studied his strong regular features, heavy black eyebrows, and dark hair. The man's foreign clothing indicated he must be Abram. His garment, with its red and blue geometric stripes, fastened over the left shoulder, allowing the right arm to be free.

Butlers and serving girls passed food in bowls of faience, gold, and silver. Perfume hung heavy in the air. Flowers in vases of silver, gold, or alabaster added to the fragrance. The serving girls kept a continuous supply of spiced wine flowing from their pitchers. Several servants passed out fresh supplies of perfume and garlands of flowers to the arriving guests. Other servants helped the guests rearrange any disordered clothing. Hagar drank in the splendor of the scene.

Soon the girls in the orchestra assembled on both sides of Sen Wosret. Double reed pipes, harps, flutes, and lyres provided the music for the dance. Hagar felt light of heart and foot as she took her place with the other dancers in front of Pharaoh and his guests.

Hagar and the other dancers accompanied the music with slow and dignified movements. As it gained momentum the dance became wilder, ending in a progression of leaps, somersaults, back flips, and handsprings. Then Hagar and the other dancers rushed to exchange places with the musicians and relaxed as Pharaoh stood.

He let his eyes wander over the crowd before he spoke. "I, Sen Wosret, ruler of the Two Lands, traveled south to cast dread on Nubia," he began his formal speech. "My army carried out the intents of my heart. They did all I commanded, repulsing the enemy. I made the boundary strong between Egypt and Nubia. A stele of red granite I set up at Semna. Because of my campaign the trade routes are protected. I'm building a string of forts along the Belly of Stones in the Nile.

"Capturing gold in Kush, I sent my chief treasurer, Ikhernofret, who grew up in the circle of my house, to carry it to Abydos. My heart is certain he will carry out my desires. Ikhernofret will restore the images of Osiris. He will beautify the temple.

"I brought back cattle of all kinds, sheep and donkeys without number. I have captured their women. I have carried off their dependents.

"My engineers made the final cut through 390 cubits of solid granite in the first cataract of the Nile. Fifty cubits wide and 40 cubits deep did they cut it. Now it can transport river craft. The channel is named 'Beautiful-are-the-ways-of Khekure.'"

"That's his throne name. I like it," Kheti whispered to Hagar.

His speech finished, Pharaoh sat down and stared straight ahead. The priests began to sing:

"Hail to you, Khekure, our Horus, and Divine of Form!
Land's protector who widens its borders,
Who unites foreign countries with his crown,
Who holds the Two Lands in his embrace,
Who subdues foreign lands with the motion of his hands,
His majestic tongue restrains Nubia,
His utterances made Asiatics flee."

Hagar saw Sen Wosret's pleasure. As she edged closer she heard him say to Abram, "During the seventh year of my reign Sirius rose in the east just before Amon Re. Then the Nile flooded and I knew it as a sign of success for me. I am Amon Re's son."

"Look, I can tell that Abram is not impressed," Kheti whispered. "Can he be greater than Sen Wosret?"

"Some of my booty," Pharaoh continued, "the cattle, sheep, and donkeys I captured, I offer to you that I may have Sarai."

Suddenly the pleasure faded from Abram's face. "My flocks and herds are more than ample. Sarai wishes to stay with her people."

Hagar saw a tall foreigner she assumed to be Abram's servant slip closer and whisper something to him. Pharaoh raised his voice. "I'll give more animals, servants, gold—even silver." The girl gasped. Silver was the most valuable substance in Egypt.

The merchant seemed to consider carefully before replying. "Yet your eyes have not even seen Sarai."

"My princes have praised her great beauty. With her as my wife your people and mine will have close ties. You will have the protection of the Pharaoh himself. I will pay a high bride price."

"Yes, it is most impressive." Yet Hagar sensed a reluctance on the foreigner's part.

"I offer you a great honor. I watch over all that is done. You are now under Pharaoh's protection."

In a voice not quite steady Abram answered, "I know. I am grateful."

"Soon I shall send the bride price to you. Then my servants will escort Sarai to the household of the women." He spoke with the full authority of an Egyptian sovereign. "See to it that all is done as I ask."

Silence prevailed. Then Pharaoh said in a kindlier and softer voice,

"You will be glad, friend Abram. You are a favorite of Pharaoh."

Kheti nudged Hagar. "Abram never said yes. Why was that?"

Hagar shrugged. "He doesn't look happy," she observed.

Ameni, one of the priests, asked the girls to perform more music. As Hagar strummed her harp she observed Pharaoh's pleasure but noticed that Abram still seemed unhappy.

The entertainment over, the guests gradually departed. Abram bid Pharaoh farewell then left with his servant.

The musicians and dancers gathered their instruments to return to the women's quarters. They chatted as they walked through the palace garden. At a turn in the path they came upon Abram and his servant. In a language Hagar did not understand, the two men conversed in low agitated tones. The girl knew that they were disturbed about something known only to them.

Sarai Brought to Pharaoh

▨▨▨▨▨▨▨▨▨▨▨▨▨▨▨▨▨▨▨▨▨▨▨▨▨▨▨▨▨

After Pharaoh entertained Abram the days began to blur to-gether for Hagar. Then one day, restless, she wandered through the women's quarters and found Kheti listening to a knot of women angrily discussing something.

"Pharaoh needs no more wives," one of them declared angrily. "He has taken enough wives from the Sand-dwellers to make all the treaties we need with them."

Hagar hastened to Kheti. "What is it? Tell me quick."

"Sarai arrives today. She'll live here."

"The sister of the merchant prince?" Hagar questioned.

"Yes, the most beautiful woman in the Two Lands," Kheti spat.

"How do you know she'll arrive today?"

"Some servants brought the news from the palace."

The girls listened to the cold voices of the other women as they angrily discussed the new developments. "Meraket's preparing rooms across from his for Sarai. Let's go see," Kheti urged.

"Why so close to the overseer? So he can protect her from the other women?"

"Maybe so."

"If she's so beautiful, she'll be Pharaoh's favorite." Suddenly Hagar stiffened and sniffed. "Smell the perfume."

The fragrance of fresh flowers and perfume wafted through the door of one of the rooms. Stepping inside, Hagar surveyed the chamber. "Everything's beautiful." She ran her fingers over the smoothness of the ebony cosmetic and jewelry boxes.

Near the beds against the far wall stood chests to store clothes.

On tables alabaster vases held flowers. Tasnek's maid placed oil lamps on tables and arranged stools and chairs in comfortable clusters. Hagar sighed, "Nakht, the room's so beautiful."

"Meraket ordered the best. It's now finished. The new wife will come before nightfall."

"But you've forgotten the god. Which one did Meraket order?"

Nakht sighed. "The new lady worships an invisible god. He has no image. Meraket ordered no gods for this room."

"Mother says Sarai's god is strong," Kheti volunteered as Meraket entered the room.

When he saw the girls, the overseer said, "Hagar, I want you to attend Sarai when she arrives."

Suddenly Hagar's heart felt heavy.

When they were outside the room Kheti grabbed Hagar's arm. "May the gods protect you if she demands much."

"Kheti, I don't want to attend her. No one likes her."

"Hagar, come with me. I must tell you a secret of my heart." The girl could barely suppress her excitement.

"It must be something important."

A smile bursting across her face, Kheti said, "Yes. Sen Wosret has arranged a marriage for me!"

Hagar stared at her friend. "Who is he?"

"He's a young priest. I'll be his first wife."

"So it's not Seni. Fortune smiles on you."

"I'll learn his name when I go with mother to visit his Majesty."

A feeling of loneliness crept into Hagar's heart. "Kheti, when you marry I'll still be here."

"Pharaoh will find you a husband."

Hagar sighed. "I'm afraid it would be Seni. He has many wives and children and is so old that he's almost dead."

"But wealthy. He could build you a beautiful tomb."

"He wouldn't live long enough. Right now I don't want a husband."

But Kheti's eyes danced as she quickly forgot Hagar's situation. "My heart's full of joy. I'll be the first in the eyes and heart of my husband. I'll own a tomb, furniture, maidservants, and menservants."

As the two girls lapsed into silence, Hagar wondered what it would be like with Kheti gone from the household of the women. With whom would she share secrets? How could she be happy for her? She said the words that she knew she must—and meant them. "Kheti, may the gods hover over you and conceal you from evil. May you provide your husband with sons in the way of our ancestors."

"I pray the gods favor me," Kheti agreed as they entered her mother's room.

Servants robed Kheti in new linen, and then placed a small beaded collar around her neck. The sleeveless dress made her brown skin stand out against the white cloth. Another maidservant hurried in to paint black kohl around the somber eyes heavily fringed with long dark lashes. Kheti's heavy black hair, crowned by a small band of gold, hung free around her shoulders.

Her dark eyes glowing, the girl glanced at Hagar. "Do I look ready for His Majesty's council chamber?"

Hagar glanced at her friend's hands as they played with the turquoise beads in her collar and then twisted the bracelets on her arm. Nervousness mingled with the excitement in Kheti's heart. Finally Hagar said, "Kheti, my eyes see your beauty. It must be like Sarai's."

"Ready?" Kheti's mother said. "Let's go."

The women's quarters were full of human sounds but Hagar never before knew such loneliness. Depression sent her to the garden as her heart struggled with this new problem. "Kheti will escape this tiresome place while I chafe under it," she told the warm wind. "Is my future a dull life as the wife of some stupid priest? Maybe I'll stay with Sarai always as her attendant. I must find Baufra."

She saw the gardener near the garden gate and hastened to him. "Baufra, why are you in the garden today?"

The old man laughed. "So my eyes can see and my ears hear."

"What do you mean?"

"You ask for my secret?"

"I know your secret. You wait to see a great beauty. They'll bring her to this gate, won't they?"

"There's no other."

"Baufra, is she"—the girl paused—"really beautiful and as fair as everybody says?"

"We'll soon know. I have heard that her caravan is not far away."

The girl glanced down and scuffed her sandal in the dust. "Meraket ordered me to attend her."

"Fortune falls on you. Learn from her. Abram is a great man. I've heard him speak. He is wise, and I respect his god. Khuni must see Abram, for he's a great merchant."

"But, Baufra, my heart bows down in distress. All delight in my life has perished. I'm"—she choked out the words—"lonely."

He studied her silently a bit. "Why?" he asked finally.

"Kheti is to marry a young priest."

He continued to look at her intently, then nodded. "I know. Let your heart fill with cheer. You too are old enough to marry."

"The women say old priest Seni wants a young wife."

"He's wealthy."

Her eyes filled with tears. "And he's old and ugly with many wives."

Suddenly he smiled. "Do the women really think Pharaoh will select you for him?"

"Probably. Baufra, does your heart say I should marry him?" Her voice choked.

His gaze drifted to the garden as they stood in silence. The man brushed his hands together as if to remove the problem. The silence grew and so did the uncertainty in Hagar's heart. Finally Baufra's eyes, now filled with sadness and sympathy, returned to her.

"Hagar, you are like a beloved daughter to me. No, my heart doesn't want you to marry Seni." He sighed. "But Pharaoh has promised him a wife from among the daughters of the royal household."

"Baufra, I'm afraid he'll choose me."

"If Sen Wosret wills it, you must. May obedience enter your heart." Another great sigh escaped her as he continued, "His majesty's coming marriage to Sarai will occupy him for a time. Don't try to glimpse into the future. Ignore the gossip you hear."

A shaft of fear stabbed her heart. The future seemed too far away to consider, and the present was a constant problem. How her heart hungered to escape the confines of the household of the women.

Abruptly she forgot about her problem as the noise of a caravan with its shouting drivers and protesting animals caught her attention.

Together with the old gardener she raced toward the entrance in time to see servants swing the gate wide and go out into the road. They watched the approaching caravan and listened to the drivers shout in a foreign tongue. Baufra chuckled. "Look, camels. They do not often visit our land."

Hagar thought the shaggy, awkward, stiff-legged, humpbacked beasts rather comical. In amazement she asked, "Do people really ride them?"

"Yes. Khuni must see them," Baufra laughed while he pulled Hagar out of the way to the garden wall.

As the camels lumbered through the gate Hagar saw their split upper lip, protruding eyes, slit nostrils, and loosely hung jaws. "They look so sad and stupid, mean and sullen. I don't like their smell."

The caravan halted as the drivers thumped the camels' knees with long staves, shouting, "Ikh, Ikh!" The animals complained and sank to the ground, groaning and whining and flapping their lips at the men if they came too close. Hagar's attention shifted from the camels to the two women riders who, aided by servants, stepped from the creatures's backs to the ground.

She guessed which one was Sarai even though both wore head coverings to protect them from the sun. When Sarai turned toward them, Hagar caught her breath. "Why, she's fairer than a princess from Mitanni." Baufra seemed not to hear her. Tall and beautiful, Sarai stood unafraid even when the camel turned its head and flapped its big lips at her. She addressed a tall young man near her in an unfamiliar tongue. A royal household servant translated the words for Baufra: "Eliezer, tell Abram El Shaddai will return me to his tent again."

Just then Meraket approached and bowed. "I'm Meraket, the Overseer of His Majesty's household of the women. He bids me welcome Princess Sarai. You honor us by your presence."

The foreign woman answered him in broken Egyptian, "Your hospitality is kind. Just a small room will do. Nindada and I will be leaving in a few days."

Meraket looked startled, then surprise flashed across his face. He opened his mouth, closed it, then opened it again to order the servants to carry in Sarai's baggage. Turning to Hagar, he commanded, "Attend Sarai. Acquaint her with the women's quarters. Go to her room and oversee the baggage." To Sarai he said, "I present Hagar, a daughter of the royal household. She'll be your attendant."

Hagar bowed. "I am at your service, my lady." Then she hastened into the apartment.

The baggage was lined up and ready to be unpacked when Meraket arrived with Sarai and her maid. "I'll have food sent to you tonight," he announced. "Anything that you need Hagar will then order for you."

Hagar dipped water into cups and shyly offered one to Sarai. "Your Highness, will you drink?"

Sarai took the cup, handed it to Nindada, and accepted the second for herself. "Hagar, call me Sarai."

Tongue-tied, the girl managed to stammer, "As you wish."

The two foreign women removed their head coverings, then Sarai began to unpack and hand clothes to Nindada to put in the chests. Hagar did not understand the language she spoke but listened just to hear the captivating voice.

The foreign woman's arms were bare to the shoulders. The graceful movements of her strong hands and fingers captivated Hagar. The girl thought they were beautiful. When she glanced at her own hands, they seemed so ordinary.

There are no royal women in the Two-Lands as beautiful, she told herself.

"Hagar," Sarai broke into the girl's thoughts, "Nindada and I need rest. Will you return later?"

"May the gods give you rest in the land of the Nile. I'm glad you'll be one of Sen Wosret's wives."

"Great is your kindness." Then, as Nakht entered with a bowl of fruit, Sarai said to the suddenly staring maidservant, "Tell me you name."

"Nakht," the servant girl stammered.

"Tell your master or mistress we gratefully accept fruit from the

Two Lands." Then the woman turned back to Hagar. "Pharaoh has many wives. I'm not worthy to become one, and I'll convince him of this."

Hagar noticed that Nakht lingered, hoping to pick up something she could tell the other women in the household.

By now it was time for the midday rest. Excusing herself, Hagar went to her room, opened her cosmetic box, took out a bronze mirror, and stared at her reflection. Until now she'd paid scant attention to her looks. She had been more interested in bits of news and gossip to share.

As she smoothed the high brows above dark eyes, she studied her face. The skin was brown, the lips red. She had never noticed her features—her high smooth forehead and strong, determined jaw. It was a strong face but not beautiful like Sarai's. Hagar examined herself more intently. Her wide-set eyes were clear, lighted by an inner fire, and her teeth were even and white. She was still young enough that the ever-present sand in Egyptian bread flour had not yet worn them down. "How can I ever look like Sarai?" she whispered to her reflection.

The voices of children leaving for the garden notified Hagar that the afternoon rest was over. She saw that Nakht's news had spread everywhere throughout the household as the women sat on chairs, stools, and the floor in Sarai's room and discussed the foreign woman's hair, skin, and eyes. "Is your brother fair too?" one woman asked.

The Sand-dweller woman smiled. "Abram's hair is dark but his eyes are gray. His skin is darker than mine but lighter than yours."

"Pharaoh likes fair women," Tasnek said, "but we have heard that you don't want to stay. Why would you not want to be wife to the greatest ruler on earth?"

An air of suspense grew as the women waited for Sarai to reply. "I wasn't born in your land," the new woman said finally. "I serve a different God who created all things. He is very great."

"But we know that god," someone interrupted. "We call him Ptah. After he created, though, some say he forgot us."

"Pharaoh built Ptah a temple in your land at Ashkelon," another added.

"We have gods closer to us," others commented. "They are friendly to Ptah."

"Sarai, add your god to ours. We serve new gods along with the ancient ones."

"I worship Amon Re with the royal court," Tasnek said. "Pharaoh is his son, so he too is a god. Here in the royal household I pray to Bes for protection for my children."

"Osiris decides our fate for eternity," someone else pointed out. "That makes him powerful."

Sarai held up a hand and all talking ceased. "My people know the Creator-God as El Shaddai. At the moment my heart is heavy for He desires me to stay with my people."

"Sarai, your heart matches your tongue but Pharaoh's god is strong," cautioned a small woman. "Is that why you don't want to be Pharaoh's wife? Every woman in our land would love to marry him."

A murmur of agreement passed through the group. Amazed, Hagar noticed they seemed to like the newcomer.

Sarai spoke again, her voice with its foreign accent commanding their attention. "El Shaddai does not want me to marry Pharaoh even though he's a great monarch. I'm loyal to my God."

"How do you know your God doesn't want you to marry Pharaoh? Did He tell you? You can't rely on the gods," someone said.

"He speaks to Abram."

"The palace will stand firm on its desire," Tasnek predicted.

A servant entered to light the lamps, breaking up the conversation. The women drifted away.

In Pharaoh's Household

The morning after Sarai's arrival Hagar toured the garden with her. Finding that the woman shared her love for gardens, she thought to herself, *This is a perfect day. My heart has forgotten its problems.*

When they returned to the veranda, Sarai said, "Hagar, sit here with me. Let's seek out each other's heart."

"The feelings of my heart come and go like the wind," Hagar said shyly, surprised that she felt so open with the foreign woman. "Yesterday saw sadness but today gladness."

Nindada handed them cups of water. Sarai drank while she studied Hagar, then asked, "What could make you sad?"

"Because my mother died at my birth, I'm inferior to the others."

"I'm sorry you missed knowing her. I'd like to have a daughter as well as a son. Our God promised my brother a son. Tell me, what have you learned while here in the household of the women?"

The girl though a moment. "I've learned the skills of music and dance. I've memorized many wise sayings of the ancients and the history of our Two Lands. From the priests I've learned about our gods."

"Do the daughters of the royal household learn to cook?"

"We learn for fun. But we also learn to supervise servants and organize households. My heart yearns for the outdoors. Baufra taught me the ways of a garden."

A smile crept into Sarai's eyes as she said, "When we were in the garden I recognized your knowledge. I will like Baufra, then. Pharaoh is fortunate to have such a wise gardener."

"Baufra's like a father. It is he who told me about Sinuhe."

"Who is Sinuhe?"

"An attendant of the wife of King Sen Wosret I who coreigned with his father Amenemhet I. There was a conspiracy in the royal household when Amenemhet's feet departed to eternity." When Sarai looked puzzled at the expression, Hagar explained, "When he died. Afraid of what might happen, Sinuhe fled to Canaan where he lived many years with the Sand-dwellers and had numerous sons. When he grew old Pharaoh let him return to be buried in a fine tomb." Hagar hesitated. Glancing at Sarai, she added, "I like the Sand-dwellers."

The woman laughed. "Sometime tell me more about Sinuhe and the Sand-dwellers. For now, tell me about Sen Wosret III."

"Sen Wosret is the son of Amon Re, the god who shines on us. Since Sen Wosret is a god, we give him obedience."

Sarai smiled. "That's why I'm here, because I obeyed, but do his people always obey him?"

"We do his commands or we die. That's why we exist."

"You've helped me." Sarai stood. "This morning the servants will fit some linen dresses for me to wear when I meet Pharaoh. Then after the heat of the day the women and I will visit here on the veranda. Will you be present, for I may need your help?"

"May I bring Kheti? She is a daughter of the royal household."

"You may." Then Sarai said something to Nindada in her own tongue.

When the afternoon rest ended Hagar and Kheti met on the veranda. Kheti's eyes sparkled. "Fortune fell on you, Hagar. Pharaoh's wives love Sarai."

Hagar nodded. "Yes, when she speaks everyone listens."

Kheti sighed. "She puts new thoughts in my heart."

Hagar cupped her hands behind her ears, "We must hold our ears open. Women like to pass time in talk, and we'll hear much." Both of them laughed.

Sarai appeared on the veranda carrying a stool. She smiled at the girls. Hagar smiled in return but wondered, *Why does she carry a stool? That's a servant's job.*

The other women began to gather, chatting all the while. Their white dresses, collared with beads or turquoise and carnelian pectorals on their chests, emphasized their dark eyes and brown skins. It contrasted with Sarai's fairer features.

Tasnek, tall, dignified, and officious, joined the group. In a display of authority she took immediate charge of the conversation. "Be at rest, everyone. Sen Wosret has gone to Dashur to inspect his pyramid. He'll not call for any of us today."

"His station in the West is firm," someone added. "He is prepared to enjoy everlasting life."

Beket, a petite and lively woman with large dark eyes, said, "I agree. He has furniture, vessels, gold, ivory and silver enough to equip his tomb."

It was not only what Sarai said in response but also how she spoke it that caught every ear. "Your magnificent tombs tell me much. You have a great desire for eternity. Does Pharaoh give lots of attention to his pyramid?"

"Oh, yes," came a chorus of answers.

Sarai looked thoughtful. "Death seems a great concern in your country. You spend more time and labor on your tombs than your dwellings. Why are you more preoccupied with death than living?"

"Because we enjoy life, we want it to continue in the afterlife," Tasnek explained. "Sen Wosret needs treasure for eternity. If his body perishes, his name disappears. His ka—his spirit—will be lost. His eternal survival depends on the preservation of his body. Don't you know that death is the key that opens the palace of eternity? Pharaoh is the son of Amon Re. He'll burst from the shell of death as a bird hatches from an egg."

"The gods will take him to the sky," added a voice from the far side of the veranda.

"His pyramid builders have already eaten a million bunches of garlic, radishes, and onions while they build Sen Wosret's House of Eternity," someone else commented. "He is well-prepared for eternity."

Hagar heard giggles before Tasnek continued. "His memory will never die. To speak the name of the dead restores the breath of life in those who have vanished."

As she listened old questions whispered in Hagar's heart. *Why do we make such vast preparations for the other world? What have the ancients done to benefit us? Did they conquer death? Are the legends true about men who spent their whole life building their tombs?*

As if reading Hagar's heart, a woman said in a puzzled voice, "Why do we leave this world for the next? Life on earth passes so quickly but being in eternity is forever."

Hagar glanced at Sarai who seemed to listen with keen interest. Then a low voice answered, "We come from darkness and return to darkness. This dark mystery embraces us for life."

"My heart burns within my chest," Beket said. "Eternity terrifies me. I'm afraid my heart will reveal its secrets in the judgment."

Somewhat shy, Nefru looked at Beket and broke into a dimpled smile. "You take thoughts from my heart. How can the heart balance with a feather of truth?"

An uneasiness formed in Hagar's heart. For the first time she recognized that all the royal women, so outwardly sure of themselves, inwardly puzzled over the riddle of life just as she did. At that moment she felt closer to them.

Tasnek replied with a ring of certainty in her voice. "Pharaoh knows magic that will equip him to stand in the judgment. His heart won't tell its secrets."

"His good deeds will be piled up in heaps by him," Meret-Neit jested.

Tasnek looked displeased but continued. "There is magic in the words the scribes write on stone. Hundreds of words piled in heaps will sit beside Sen Wosret in his tomb. I've seen some of them. They say:

"'I have not mistreated cattle.
I have not made anyone sick.
I have not made anyone weep.
I have not killed.
I have not defiled myself.
I have not made anyone unhappy.'"

Hearing this, Iput, whose private thoughts often leaked out through her tongue, interrupted, "Then why is there unhappiness in the household of the women?" Laughter rippled through the group.

Again ignoring the interruption, Tasnek went on quoting:

" 'I stand well with people.
I gave bread to the hungry.
I clothed the naked.
I am silent with the angry.
I am patient with the ignorant.' "

Is Sen Wosret really that good? Hagar wondered. Then she remembered something Baufra had once said: "Every Pharaoh's faults are written in the waters of the Nile. His virtues are in stone."

Beket spoke again. "My heart is full of questions. The ancients built their tombs but now their places are gone. What has become of them? I feel trapped and controlled by outside forces."

When she finished silence hovered over the group. When no one else said anything, Beket said, "Let me quote a wise man:
" 'I have heard the words
Of Imhotep and Hardedef,
Whose sayings are recited whole.
What of their places?
Their walls are crumbled,
Their places are gone
As though they had never been.
None come from there
To tell their state,
To tell of their needs,
To calm our hearts
Until we go where they have gone!' "

"My heart is full of fire," Kheti whispered to Hagar. "Is the Field of Reeds, the afterworld, only a dream?"

In the silence that followed Hagar studied the faces around her. It seemed as if each woman struggled with disturbing thoughts—as if they felt themselves at the mercy of the unknown. Hagar glanced at Sarai who sat with hands in her lap, troubled furrows between her eyes.

"The priests are masters of secrets in the temples," Tasnek said authoritively. "They control everything. Let's not cover our faces in fear of tomorrow. You should see Pharaoh's mortuary boats, five of them. Shu, god of air, will lift Sen Wosret and all his treasures up to

35

the wide stairway of heaven. Then he will sail on the winding waters of the celestial sky to Lightland. There Amon Re takes a morning bath in the Field of Rushes. Sen Wosret will bathe in the company of Amon Re. We'll speak the name of Sen Wosret to restore the breath of life in him when he has vanished. He will still be in eternity as generation succeeds generation. His Ba and his Ka will know the way to the portal that conceals the dead." She lapsed into silence.

Curious, Sarai said, "I don't understand. What are the Ba and Ka?"

"The priests say the Ba is the life force that leaves the body at death," Nefru explained. "The body will decay unless it is embalmed. Sometimes the Ba returns to a preserved body it knows. The Ka is like a shadow, a double, a vital force or personality. It is our total heart—our thoughts and physical properties. It is us, our character."

Again Tasnek spoke emphatically. "Sen Wosret is a god, son of Amon Re. He will have no trouble in eternity."

Hagar swallowed hard to hide her nervousness. Did she, a young girl, dare to speak her radical thoughts to these older women? Gathering courage and trying to imitate Sarai's regal tone, she said, "Sen Wosret is like a man but numbered among the gods, yet forced to kneel before them. He inspects buildings, he hunts, he robes himself, he eats and sleeps like any man. Death can come to him in battle. He worships Amon Re. But if he is also Amon Re, does he worship himself?"

Stunned, the women stared at her. Hagar gulped, then glanced at Sarai and saw her eyes wide with astonished admiration.

Nefru adroitly changed the subject. "Sarai, you have the manners of the well-born. Yet you live with Sand-dwellers who bury their dead in sheep skins or fold them up in jars. Why?"

"I was born in Ur. They buried treasure with their dead as you do here. I have walked through the lands of many people. But now I see Amon Re is about to leave the sky. May I tell you tomorrow after rest time what I know about death, eternity, and burial customs?"

"Yes, do," the women chorused.

As the others left the veranda Hagar silently explored her thoughts. She had spent her early years with a people who loved life and imagined no better existence beyond the grave than the one they enjoyed on earth. Yet often her heart questioned their fantastic beliefs. She did not understand why she felt herself drawn to Sarai more than any other person in her entire life. Was it because the woman did not use her beauty to seek advantage against the other women? Could it be her kindness, her treatment of servants as equals, or her obvious love of children? The Sand-dweller woman seemed to have something that Hagar didn't understand. Did it relate to her own longing for a mother? Whatever the reason, she knew that she wanted to share a friendship with this woman of another country, another race, and of a different age.

Hagar's thoughts returned to the veranda as suddenly she realized that she and Kheti were alone with Sarai.

"Sarai," Hagar hesitated, then said eagerly, "may we get Meraket's permission to take you down to the Nile to see Amon Re rise in the morning? We'd have to leave while it is yet dark."

The older woman's smile widened and her eyes sparkled. "I'd like to see it. I'll meet you here in the morning."

Hagar and Kheti remained on the veranda, talking until the stars began to appear.

El Shaddai

🔲🔲🔲🔲🔲🔲🔲🔲🔲🔲🔲🔲🔲🔲🔲🔲🔲🔲🔲🔲🔲🔲🔲🔲🔲🔲🔲🔲🔲🔲🔲

Just before dawn Hagar heard some donkeys bray and Pharaoh's pet lion roar. In a flash she remembered that she and Kheti had planned to show Sarai and her maid the beauty of the Nile at Amon Re's rising.

Just then servants entered with lamps and water. After she bathed they rubbed perfumed oil into Hagar's skin, then slipped a white linen dress over her head and braided her hair. Finished, Hagar hurried to the veranda to meet Kheti, Sarai, and Nindada. As they inhaled the cool morning air they drew their shawls closer around them.

The path they chose led around the women's palace, through a gate at which a guard waved them on, and down to the edge of the river. Hagar marveled at the ease with which Sarai and the elderly Nindada managed the terraced bank. *Sarai's mouth isn't obsessed with her station in life as a princess,* she thought. *More than blood recommends her.*

Slowly the stars faded in the brightening sky and the dawn gently roused the earth. Silhouettes of serrated palms held up the vaulted sky. Hagar divided her attention between Sarai's delight at the scene and the unfolding morning itself.

Far across the river shadowy figures of men straddled donkeys and women balanced water jugs on their heads. Then as the sky grew lighter, green fields and patches of plowed earth became visible. From the village of dried mud-brick houses came faint squalls of hungry babies. Above the distant hills traces of pink announced Amon Re's approach. An expectant hush close to reverence seemed suspended in the air. It stirred in Hagar a loneliness and a longing akin to worship.

They watched the edge of the gilded sphere of the sun rise above the horizon and climb higher to a full circle of grandeur. Then a north wind rippled the reflection of Amon Re's light on the surface of the broad river. As the golden orb crested the sky-line of palms the Nile became a silver ribbon, banded by green flowing into the distance. "Sarai, it's like infinity or life everlasting," Hagar said. The shadows of the pyramids retreated as the desert turned bronze and Amon Re vanquished the last bit of dawn into full day.

A long sigh escaped Sarai. "Beautiful," she said. "The Nile gives life to the desert." Then more to herself than to the others, she added, "It must be like the first garden that El Shaddai made. I feel so close to He who created this beautiful morning."

"But Amon Re created this morning," Kheti protested.

"True." The glow of Sarai's smile radiated in all directions as kindness guided her tongue. "But El Shaddai made Amon Re."

The shouts of sailors as they loaded their boats at the palace docks caught their attention. "Pharaoh will go duck hunting in the papyrus marshes today and will take with him musicians, atten-dants, and servants," Kheti informed Sarai.

Sarai and Nindada began to converse in their strange tongue, pointing as they became more excited. Turning to Hagar, Sarai said, "I see Abram and Eliezer. They will straighten things out with Sen Wosret." Then she resumed her conversation with her servant.

Hagar met Kheti's confused eyes. "Is Sarai's God more powerful than Amon Re?" Kheti asked.

"I don't know, but Sarai seems so confident." Hagar fell silent and began to ponder what she had just said.

In midafternoon, while the children were in the garden, the women gathered on the veranda. As they shared news and gossip Hagar studied them. To her beauty had always been clothing, cos-metics, and jewelry, but now she studied their physical features and heard the music in their cultured voices. "You are favored to attend her," Kheti said as she noticed Hagar glancing at Sarai.

"Yes, my status in the royal household is higher because of her."

"Stay with us," Beket said to Sarai.

"Once Sarai sees Pharaoh she'll stay," Tasnek commented. "You can't say no to Sen Wosret."

Sarai smiled. "I must obey El Shaddai," she replied simply.

Nefru stood and moved to sit closer to Sarai. "You promised to give us your knowledge of death and eternity."

"Your wisdom is well known," Tasnek said. "The words of your mouth will please our ears."

Hagar and Kheti joined the chorus. "Let your mouth speak. Our ears are open to listen."

Sarai's glance circled the room. "We all speak the same heart language, only our words are different. Will you help me if I need the right word in your language?"

"Yes," several offered, "but you are skilled in our tongue."

Sarai began to speak, her hands molding words when her tongue hesitated. "El Shaddai, the creator, spoke to Abram saying, 'Leave Ur your home and go to a land I will show you.' More than 1,000 servants and retainers went with us. We traveled many weeks and months, met new people, and found different customs. In Haran and Canaan we learned to speak some of the Akkadian, Egyptian, and Amorite tongues.

"In your country you call your creator-god Ptah, but in Sumerian, the language of Ur, he is called Enlil, and in my language El Shaddai. In Ur the priests and rulers have gained power and wealth for themselves by planting a fear of the gods in people. Priests, kings, and storytellers have distorted for their own purposes the history of the Creator and His power to save humanity for eternity. They weave fanciful webs from their own imaginations. As a result the Sumerians try to redeem themselves."

When Sarai paused as if in thought, Tasnek asked, "Are their tombs as splendid as ours here in the Two Lands?"

"No, but they place many things in their tombs for a future life. In times past the kings had their families and servants killed and buried in their tombs with them. Death is a human problem," she continued. "We all face it. But that was not so when El Shaddai created the first man and woman."

"I've heard He put them in a garden," Beket interrupted.

"Right," Sarai agreed. "El Shaddai created them in His image and gave them authority to make decisions for themselves. In my language we call the man Ish and the woman Ishshah. El Shaddai formed Ish from dust and Ishshah from a rib of Ish. He gave them breath, or a spark of life. In their garden home El Shaddai planted a special tree. Then He warned Ish and Ishshah that if they chose to eat of its fruit they would know evil, which results in death." She paused.

Hagar saw the women's intense interest as Sarai continued. "A created being tried to place himself above El Shaddai. He struggled to usurp the High God, as in your story of when Seth killed Osiris and tried to steal the rulership of the gods from Horus. When his selfish plan failed in heaven, he then visited the garden and spoke through a serpent to Ishshah. He said, 'You will not die. The fruit of this tree will make you very wise.' His words persuaded Ishshah to eat the fruit, and she gave some to Ish, who also ate. Wrong choices have within themselves the seeds of destruction, so their decision plunged them down the path to death. Thus death became the birthright of their descendants. As a result people became captives and slaves to their wrong choices."

"Their deeds placed the land in pain and anguish," Beket declared.

"And filled hearts with death and despair," Nefru added.

"You understand well," Sarai agreed. "From that first wrong choice has flowed a history of pain, suffering, and tears. We're only pieces of clay or mud with a spark of life. When the breath is gone we die and turn back to dust."

Meret-Neit laughed. "We're well-colored clay. But, Sarai, your clay has no color." Laughter filled the room at her comment, and Sarai joined with them.

What the Sand-dweller woman had said raised questions in Hagar's heart. "Why don't the priests capture the spark of life, tie it down, imprison it, so we won't die?" she blurted.

Tasnek agreed with her. "The priests must find a way. Long ago we discovered how to mummify the body to keep it from turning to dust." Others nodded but Hagar was also aware of raised brows and shrugs.

Then she saw the priest, Ameni, ascend the veranda stairs. Hagar

41

knew well the gossip that Ameni worshiped wealth as well as his gods. Tasnek turned to him. "Ameni, Priest of Amon Re, welcome. Sarai speaks about death and eternity. Will you stay?"

Hagar saw the priest's shrewd glance directed toward Sarai. "My business is with Meraket. May Pharaoh's royal wives enjoy Princess Sarai."

After Ameni disappeared into the women's palace, Sarai continued. "Eating the forbidden fruit changed the nature of Ish and Ishshah. It became easier for them and for succeeding generations to make wrong choices.

"Ish and Ishshah grieved over the anguish their decisions brought to the heart of El Shaddai. They longed for righteousness—for, as you would say, ma'at—and wanted forgiveness and help for any future struggle with the power of choice. Their hearts filled with anguish, because the rebellious being controlled everything.

"After many long lifetimes humanity gained much knowledge and learned to produce many wonderful things. However, people didn't love God or each other so they filled the world with violence. El Shaddai then decided to permit a supreme catastrophe, a worldwide flood, to destroy almost all life. Unlike the inundation of your Nile, it spread over all the land. But God found a righteous man to build an ark to save his family and a few animals and birds. The flood destroyed the earth."

"Will there be another such flood?" someone asked.

Sarai shook her head. "El Shaddai said, no, not one that big ever again."

Hagar noticed Meraket and Ameni talking in the hall. They seemed to be paying as much attention to Sarai as they did to each other. Again Hagar returned her attention to Sarai. "Let's forget the flood for the moment and go back to the beginning," the foreign woman said. "Sorrow flowed from the heart of El Shaddai for He loved Ish and Ishshah whom He had created. The mantle of grief weighed heavily on Him since death would mean eternal separation from Ish and Ishshah. It was the kind of death your people call the second death when Amemait the devourer slays those who fail the test of the feather of Ma'at in the Judgment Hall of Osiris. El Shaddai told Ish and Ishshah, 'I'll provide a substitute. He will pay the penalty of eternal death. In the future He'll be born to a woman. When He becomes a man He'll win the right to save all who choose to follow Him.'"

"But death isn't eternal in Egypt either," Tasnek interrupted. "Our past pharaohs are already stars in the sky. They watch over us."

"Sen Wosret is a god born of a woman," Iput said. "Will he take death away?"

"Your hearts are full of questions, I know," Sarai said. "The substitute of whom I speak, however, has not yet been born. El Shaddai instructed Ish and Ishshah to slay a lamb and sacrifice it on an altar to remind them of the future death of their Substitute."

"I like El Shaddai," Beket said. "The One He promises to send is like Osiris who came to life after he died and who gives us eternal life."

"Did El Shaddai kill His enemy who caused Ishshah to eat the fruit?" Iput asked.

"No, the evil one rebelled against the government of heaven and was cast out. El Shaddai is fair and would have paid the penalty for even this one's wrong choices but the evil one was not sorry. He claimed that he was right in all that he did and said. Instead his claims have broken the heart of the world. El Shaddai does not force His way on others. He is giving the evil one time to show how his plan works. Because Ishshah and Ish yielded to him, the evil one now has great power in the world, but it won't always be so."

Tasnek leaned toward Sarai. " Egypt has a serpent-like adversary of the gods, Apophis. He acts like the evil one you describe. Each day Amon Re crushes and repels him as he rides across the sky."

Nefru sighed as if a weight had lifted from her heart. "Then eternity is possible. I want it."

"But it is not for all. Remember the judgment," Merit-Neit reminded. A murmur of objection rose from the women.

Hagar thought about what Sarai had said. *Sometimes I listen to my heart and long to find something. But what?*

"Sarai speaks with such assurance," Hagar whispered to Kheti. "I want Sarai's wisdom."

Sarai's eyes misted over and in a voice filled with emotion she said, "The Creator cannot be identified with the sun, moon, river, mountains, wind, rain, human beings, or any creature. His name—whether it be Ptah, Enlil, or El Shaddai—signifies an all-powerful eternal being."

Servants now arrived with water for the women. As Hagar sipped some she saw Ameni slip down the stairs and walk toward the palace. She shuddered for he made her remember the old priest Seni.

"Sarai, do you have an image of El Shaddai?" Nefru asked.

"No one could make an image of clay, wood, or stone to represent Him in the right way. He is light, so the image of El Shaddai must be in the heart."

The royal wives sat in a strained silence until Beket said wistfully, "It would be so much easier to worship just one god."

"What would all the priests do if we served only one?" Iput demanded.

A palace messenger bounded up the stairs and bowed before Sarai. "Pharaoh requests an audience with you in his council chamber. He would have you see his countenance and will send for you in the morning."

The women began to murmur among themselves as they entered their palace. In the reception hall Hagar overheard one of the wives remark that "Sarai has fire in her heart."

Her companion replied, "It's not her words so much, it's her voice and the way she looks and talks. She is so sure about El Shaddai."

"The priests would not be happy to worship just one god," another remarked. "I wonder if we have so many gods because of them."

Hagar knew she shouldn't allow her thoughts to jump around the way they were doing. She felt a twinge of shame and disloyalty because she realized her admiration for Sarai was greater than for the other women. As they discussed what they had heard, they skimmed the surface of Sarai's words but did not reach to the heart of them.

Suddenly Hagar's pulse hammered in her throat. She liked El Shaddai. He must be full of love.

Before Pharaoh

Hagar and Meraket bowed before Prince Marasar. Then the overseer said, "We bring you Sarai. Pharaoh expects the merchant Abram's sister. Take her to him."

Marasar studied Sarai with interest. "Come, Pharaoh is waiting."

Remaining at a discreet distance but near enough to see and hear, Hagar and Meraket followed them into the audience chamber. There she saw her father, whom she scarcely knew, sitting on a magnificent throne upon a raised dais. Two Nubian fan-bearers with their ostrich plumed fans stood on each side along with royal princes arrayed in the uniforms of high-ranking army officers. Court officials, scribes, and priests were seated below the dais to record the proceedings, offer counsel, or execute Pharaoh's commands.

Pharaoh's red and white headdress curved behind his close-set ears and fell forward in front of his shoulders. His large collar of red, yellow, blue, and white beads contrasted with his brown skin. A matching beaded belt held in place his pleated white skirt of crisply-folded linen. Leather sandals protected his feet.

Hagar looked closer at the finely chiseled face, the long slender nose and sensitive lips. She knew by reputation he was a likable man with a strong heart of love, but one who expected results. His people saw him as a fearless warrior and bold hunter. He was one who wanted to triumph every time, whether in battle or palace intrigue. If he didn't win, he could be very cruel.

Marasar and Sarai advanced to a position before the throne. The young prince saluted with raised arm. "O great Pharaoh Sen Wosret, Son of Amon Re, Ruler of Upper and Lower Egypt, Bearer of the

Throne Name Khekure, I bring to stand before you the prince Abram's sister, Sarai. You sent for her."

Hagar noticed that, in contrast to the royal power displayed around her, Sarai appeared defenseless. But Hagar also sensed an inner strength in her that set her apart. All eyes around Pharaoh focused on the splendid woman. Silently Pharaoh examined the stately Sand-dweller.

With mounting surprise and admiration Hagar watched the encounter. Calm and unafraid Sarai stood before him without even averting her eyes. She looked up at Pharaoh as if to measure the man, to probe the very depths of his character. In uneasy silence Hagar continued to hold her breath as she watched Pharaoh become unnerved. Sarai, not Pharaoh, seemed to be in charge. He struggled to regain his composure, then said, "My princes describe you as fair—fair as the morning star. They praise your conduct and manners. Now I see you are made to be a queen, to sit beside me. Let your tongue speak."

Sarai kept her gaze on the king. It was as if she felt alone with him. Taking a step forward, she declared, "Mighty Khekure, Ruler of the Two Lands, Double Lord, it was you who sent for me. Is it not you who wish to speak?"

"Your tongue speaks well in the language of Egypt. But Meraket the overseer of the palace of the women reports your heart is not happy with the great honor Pharaoh bestows on you. Why?"

"Great Khekure, I serve El Shaddai, the Creator. It's not His will that I enter your household. I wish to return to Abram's camp."

Hagar saw surprised annoyance flit across her father's face as he replied, "Sarai, don't vex my heart. The world's strongest gods dwell here in Egypt. When my people come into my presence they bow down to worship me, for I too am a god." Sen Wosret shifted on the throne to a stiffer position. "My spirit is indestructible. As my fathers in the pyramids continue to live for me, I speak the truth. Whom I wish to live, lives. Who I wish to die, dies. I bring my enemies down to dust and their name is forgotten. They will be as though they never were."

"Mighty Khekure, Double Lord of the Two Lands, your fortresses, colonies, and trade routes cause your language to be much spoken in Canaan." Sarai pointed to her ears then spread her hands and arms. "Our ears heard of your good roads, your caravansaries, your water and grass, your fields laden with grain. We learned of your mines and smelters, which produce tools of bronze. And we know you are kind to foreigners. All these things brought us to Egypt. Because there was no rain, Canaan was bowed down in distress. Our flocks and herds melted before our eyes!"

"I am a king who speaks and acts. What my heart plans, my arm accomplishes." Pharaoh rose to emphasize his words and spread his arms wide. "Welcome. You will find that Egypt sustains life. I have extended the boundary of my land further south than my fathers. I am one who attacks to conquer, one who is swift to succeed, one in whose heart a plan does not slumber."

"Plan? Mighty Khekure, when does the plan to return me to Abram begin?"

Hagar watched Pharaoh's face darken. His eyes narrowed and blazed with indignation as he sought to gain time. "Not all that one's heart pleads for can be granted. Sarai, a black goat-hair tent in the land of the Sand-dwellers cannot compare with a palace in Egypt. As the wife of Pharaoh you will have a magnificent tomb decked with gold, a ceiling of lapis lazuli, walls of silver, doors of copper with bolts of brass. Your name will go forth even after your mouth is silent. But with Abram you will go to the house of death in a sand pit, your bones wrapped in a ram's skin. Your memory will be as though it had never been. Our gods have decreed that you should be in Pharaoh's palace."

"But Pharaoh Khekure, El Shaddai has not decreed these things." Sarai refused to back down.

Hagar froze as Pharaoh almost shouted, "I am a god, I can do no wrong. Who is this God who dares oppose Pharaoh and the gods of Egypt?"

Every nerve tense, Hagar listened as Sarai answered, "His name is El Shaddai. He is no mere Canaanite god of wood or stone, but the Creator of the heavens and the earth and all that is in them." Sarai's voice had a self-assurance that held everyone's attention as

47

she continued, "He has promised to come to the earth in the form of humanity to deliver His people from the bondage of wrong-doing. El Shaddai will judge the world and be its king, caring for His people as a shepherd does his sheep."

Pharaoh gasped. "You speak with the tongue of Ipuwer."

She looked puzzled. "Ipuwer? Who is Ipuwer?"

"In the days of my grandfathers Ipuwer foretold of a savior who will restore the land. He proclaimed the coming of a good king of whom humanity shall say, 'He is the shepherd of all the people; there is no evil in his heart.' Do you speak of this king?"

"Perhaps Ipuwer spoke of El Shaddai, the God who knows your heart and mine. Whether he did or not, I don't know, but this I do know: El Shaddai does not want me to become your wife."

Hagar heard Pharaoh's angry sigh, saw his strong mouth twitch. "Sarai, for you I have paid Abram countless sheep, cattle, donkeys, camels, and many servants. I have provided rooms in the palace where he may stay when he visits. He will be favored by me. My servants will cook meals for him in my own dinner-pots."

Sarai shook her head. "Pharaoh Khekure, I cannot accept the honor you bestow. Abram will return everything. In your royal household you have many beautiful women. Why do you need another?"

Hagar sensed her father's restrained anger and noticed a growing uneasiness among those present in the throne room. Her alarm for Sarai grew. Would Pharaoh regard the woman as being insolent and execute her?

With measured calm Pharaoh replied, "I am weary of them. You are a woman of great learning like Neferu-koyt and her mother who lived in ancient times. Like them, you are educated, wise, and beautiful. You are not afraid of me and show yourself equal to a man. In some women that is a pleasing trait. You would be a favorite wife, a mother of kings, a model for the children of the great. Sarai, I implore you to fill my palace with children, sons succeeding sons."

"Mighty Khekure, once again, I cannot accept the honor you offer. I want to worship my God with my people." Her voice was powerful, and she had a way of emphasizing words.

Pharaoh studied her with renewed determination, then replied carefully, "I have tested your heart in conversation. Your heart matches your tongue. Time will stir your heart and make you desire me." Pharaoh watched the effect of his words on the silent, calm Sarai before he continued. "Then the officials will say Sarai was wise to bend her back to her superior. I am a great man, strong and handsome. There is none equal to me. Let my speech fall on your heart like fire."

Hagar saw the amazement of the palace officials. Sarai herself did not move except to lift her hand to her throat as the Egyptian ruler fell silent. The girl watched both her father and Sarai. Her heart spoke with two voices. Her Egyptian nature wanted Pharaoh's court to consider him master of the encounter, and the feminine part of her pleaded that the dignified Sarai remain in the household of the women and not be intimidated by Pharaoh.

As Sarai and Pharaoh measured each other a prolonged, intense silence blanketed the audience chamber. Then Pharaoh blinked. Nodding almost imperceptibly to Meraket, the king said forcefully, "Sarai, remain in the harem."

Sit-Hathor-Yunet

██

Hagar looked in her mirror. Her makeup and clothes had become more mature in the short time she'd been attending Sarai. After fingering the bead collar and admiring the whiteness of the linen dress that she had donned especially to visit the palace, she hurried to Sarai's chamber. Then together they went through the garden to the path leading to the palace. A guard met and escorted them to the living quarters of Pharaoh's sister.

Scattered here and there in the reception room were carved animal-leg tables and chairs. Fragrant flowers filled gold and alabaster vases. Bright life-size paintings covered two walls. On another wall a finely decorated window framed the outdoor garden. Nearby a door led to a veranda from which one could see a long expanse of the Nile. Here each morning the princess watched Amon Re rise. The fourth wall was decorated with an hieroglyphic inscription, and a large arched doorway led to the rest of the apartment. Hagar, seeing Sarai's interest in the room, said, "If you become Pharaoh's favorite, you could become the royal mother and have an apartment like this."

"Oh Hagar, you don't understand," Sarai replied sadly. "I'd rather live in Abram's tents."

In the arched doorway the petite princess appeared and hesitated. Behind her in the hall stood several attendants. Adorned as though she expected someone important, Sit-Hathor-Yunet wore a long sleeveless dress. The white linen set off her smooth olive skin. The beads in her necklace, girdle, and bracelets consisted of amethyst, turquoise lapis lazuli, carnelian, and gold. The pectoral, or

50

plate, she wore on her breast was a gift from Sen Wosret II. In the center a cartouche bore his name.

A wide gold band decorated with gold sculptured flowers circled her dark hair, and a gold cobra fastened to the band rose from the middle of her forehead. The royal uraeus, or sacred snake, had a head of lapis lazuli, eyes of garnet, and a hood ornamented with cornelian, turquoise, and lapis lazuli. Thick strands of gold and ebony beads hung all around from the band except in front of her face, and they reached well below her shoulders. She walked through the arch wafting a cloud of costly fragrance.

Hagar had long admired the woman, who was a palace favorite. She watched Sit-Hathor-Yunet approach them, her velvet, khol-lined eyes on Sarai. Stepping forward, Hagar bowed. "Princess Sit-Hathor-Yunet, sister of Pharaoh Sen Wosret, I present princess Sarai, sister of merchant prince Abram."

"Welcome, princess Sarai. My brother's eyes are taken with your beauty. But then no wonder, so are mine. He says you are also wise."

Sarai smiled warmly in return. "To be your guest is a great honor to me, a Sand-dweller."

"Come, let us talk with each other. I like the way you speak our language." Sit-Hathor-Yunet led her to chairs near a low table while Hagar joined the princess's attendants as they went for refreshments.

"Is it true she doesn't get angry with her servants?" one of them leaned over and whispered to Hagar.

"Sarai treats servants as equals," Hagar replied with a touch of pride in her voice.

"Then may Pharaoh let her live in the palace," another said.

They returned to the reception room with platters of grapes and sliced melon picked early that morning. As they placed the platters before the two women, Sarai smiled her appreciation. Hagar noticed that the Sand-dweller and Pharaoh's sister seemed to enjoy each other. Although she took her place with the other attendants on the far side of the room, she still carefully listened to Sarai and Sit-Hathor-Yunet's conversation.

"The melons of Egypt are especially sweet," Sarai said.

Sit-Hathor-Yunet pointed toward the Nile. "We have Hapy,

the god of the inundation, and the god Amon Re to ensure such good melons."

"Egypt resembles no other country I've seen," Sarai commented. "There's not another nation like it."

"Egypt's gods gave us a unique land. Sen Wosret is a great pharaoh, a conqueror. As the son of Amon Re he has caused Egypt to prosper."

"That's why we chose to visit Egypt when the drought struck Canaan."

The Egyptian woman looked at Sarai, then on impulse stretched out her hand and touched her. "Become one of us. My brother desires you. He says you are wise as well as beautiful."

Hagar held her breath as Sarai did not reply for a moment. In an impersonal voice the woman said, "El Shaddai, my God, prefers that I stay with the Sand-dwellers."

Sit-Hathor-Yunet studied her for several minutes. "In three days we leave for Abydos to see the Passion Play of Osiris. I invite you to accompany me as my guest."

"I've heard of the great drama of Osiris."

"You'll see the power of Egypt's gods. Your El Shaddai will see and feel their power."

"You honor me by inviting me. I will go with you. As we travel may I tell you about El Shaddai? I'll be learning about your gods, and in turn I could tell you about mine."

"That would please me. I've heard of your God through the palace servants, but I'd like to have you tell me yourself."

When the king's sister stood, Hagar knew the visit had ended. "You do me great honor, Sit-Hathor-Yunet," Sarai said. "I'll be with you in three days."

"Sarai, I share my brother's good impression of you. I look for the day when you are part of our household."

Outside in the palace garden Hagar saw a jasmine bush with a solitary blossom. Picking it, she offered it to Sarai. "Here, smell the first jasmine." The woman did but her thoughts seemed somewhere else. She did not comment on the fragrance nor on the kittens scampering near the path. A little breeze from the Nile played across their faces.

Not until they were back in the garden of the household of women did Sarai speak. "Hagar, you heard Pharaoh's sister invite me to the Mystery Festival of Osiris?"

"Yes. It's the greatest drama in Egypt. Someday I want to see it."

"You will see it in a few days as my attendant."

Hagar gasped. "Oh, Sarai, can this be happening to me? Aren't you excited?"

"My excitement doesn't equal yours. A heavy problem weighs on my heart. I search for its solution."

"What problem?" the girl asked in surprise.

"The palace continues to expect me to marry Pharaoh."

"Won't you?"

"No." She sighed. "It can never be." Hagar saw tears slide down her cheeks as she turned to enter the palace of the women.

Bewildered, Hagar retreated to the fragrance of growing things. She saw Baufra near the lotus pool. "Good. My heart needs his wise words of wisdom," she mumbled to herself.

A brief smile touched his face as he sang out, "Welcome to the young lady dressed in finery, loved of the gods."

Hagar bowed. "Baufra, you tease a maiden in great distress."

"Have you dressed for a banquet?"

"I attended Sarai to Sit-Hathor-Yunet's apartment."

"So honors exceeding those of your ancestors come to you."

The girl bit her lip. "Baufra, trouble eats at my heart."

He studied her face and gestured helplessly. "Honored one, attendant to Sarai, how can you be sad?"

"I am troubled for my mistress."

"Sarai? But why?"

"She refuses to become wife to Pharaoh."

His eyes flashed as he slammed his right fist into his left hand. "Not marry Pharaoh? First you say you won't marry Seni. Now Sarai refuses to become the wife of the monarch of Egypt. What's this world coming to? Women can't decide such matters. Who ever heard such nonsense?"

"It's true," she said, suddenly frightened at his reaction.

"What's wrong with Sen Wosret? He's not old and ugly. Any

woman would be honored to marry the divine son of Amon Re."

Hagar nervously licked her lips. "Her God says that she cannot."

"The one known as El Shaddai?"

"Yes. Do you know about Him?"

"I have heard Abram speak of Him."

"Baufra, Sarai told the royal wives about Him. He seems to be a good God."

The old gardener thought a moment. "Hagar learn all you can about El Shaddai."

"I already know that He made people and breath for their noses so they can live."

He nodded. "And Abram says that He made the sky, earth, and water. But how can that be? Ptah and Amon Re brought the world into being."

"Sarai says that He will save people for eternity."

"Uh-huh. And Abram declares that El Shaddai will make death disappear."

The girl searched her memory. "According to Sarai, El Shaddai gave women as well as men the power to choose . . ."

Hagar paused as she saw hesitation in the old man's dark eyes. She sensed he did not agree. But he replied cautiously, "Not always. Some individuals have a strong hold over others." It was not what she thought he'd say, though.

Then Hagar threw caution to the winds. "My heart burns within when Sarai speaks about her God."

"You admire Sarai." Was it a statement or a question?

The girl took a breath. "Yes. She is admired by everyone. Since she came 20 days ago the women no longer quarrel like they always did. Now they're kind to the servants. Nor are the women jealous of her as they usually are toward new wives."

He was silent for a long time. "A fine woman," he said finally. "Hagar, mold your character after hers."

"Baufra, is her God powerful?"

"Yes, I believe He is."

"More powerful than Egypt's gods?"

"My heart says yes." The words came reluctantly and he sighed.

She tried to find the right way to phrase the thought that suddenly disturbed her. "What would happen to me if I didn't worship Egypt's gods?"

"Hagar, others in Egypt worship foreign gods." Strange emotions seemed to war in his expression. "One could almost believe that if El Shaddai is genuine, then our gods might be impostors."

Shocked, she protested, "But Sen Wosret is a god."

Baufra hesitated again, breaking a twig in tiny pieces. With a tone in his voice she'd never heard before, he said, "Hagar, what we have said must be for our ears alone. Keep these words buried in your heart. Sen Worset may be deceived. He may be a mere man."

The girl gasped. She would not dare to say such things even to Kheti. How could Baufra let such words escape his mouth? Nervously she changed the subject. "Sit-Hathor-Yunet asked Sarai to go to Abydos in three days."

"To see Osiris?"

"Yes. It does not thrill her heart but excitement fills mine. I'll attend her there."

"Does Sit-Hathor-Yunet push Sarai to marry Pharaoh?"

"Yes."

His mouth tightened. "There may be a real problem here." Baufra sat down on the edge of the pool. Hagar remained standing to protect her clothes. As silence wrapped them together Hagar felt this wise man to be the best and most trusted of her adult friends. Pensively she watched the frogs slide in and out of the lotus pool.

Finally the silence grew too much for her. "Why does El Shaddai say no to marriage with Pharaoh?"

"That's a puzzle, Hagar; something we don't know."

"What do you mean?"

"I hear people say that Abram is not enthusiastic about Sarai's marriage to Sen Wosret. That is strange since he has received great wealth for her. And Ameni and the other priests grumble that the bride price was too high. Keep your ears and eyes open."

Mystery Festival

Hagar waited in Sit-Hathor-Yunet's boat, watching the dancing reflection of the half moon mirrored in the water. Meanwhile servants heaped baggage on the deck, attendants fussed at each other, and the oarsmen awaited orders as governors, priests, scribes, palace personnel, and royal family members found their places aboard the flotilla of ships.

Impulsively Hagar hugged Kheti. "My heart jumps with joy."

"Why?"

"Because Meraket chose you to help attend Sarai in Abydos."

As they waited Amon Re ushered in the day and the priest's song of praise rang out over the river. Then with a gentle north wind against the sails and with the oarsmen at their posts they followed Pharaoh's royal barge south.

The pyramids receded in the distance. White Ibises perched on one leg in the fields along the river, and merchant boats crowded the middle of the Nile. Hagar plucked at her harp. "Kheti, do you feel all this life around you?"

"Let scribes ink it on my heart. I'll remember this forever."

"Sit-Hathor-Yunet, those reeds are three times as tall as a man," the girls heard Sarai exclaim.

"Those are papyrus reeds."

"In Canaan we'd make them into mats and baskets."

"My people also weave mats, baskets and crates, and twist ropes and knot sandals from papyrus. We use it to fashion boats and furniture and even eat its roots. Truly it is a gift from the gods."

"And scribes write on it?"

"Yes. It's beaten into sheets on which scribes copy the words of the gods. That is our name for writing. We use papyrus to record both His majesty's deeds and trading records."

"Does Egypt trade papyrus in the Mine-Lands and in Canaan?"

"Yes, Sen Wosret has extended trade routes to all those lands."

"Abram plans to use papyrus scrolls for his records when he returns to Canaan. It's a wonderful invention." Sarai spread her arms. "You have so much water for reeds to grow in."

Sit Hathor Yunet agreed. "Each year the Nile floods, watering our land, then a new year begins. In Sen Wosret's seventh year Sirius rose in Amon Re's path on day 16 of the fourth month of the sprouting season. At the same time the river flooded. It was a fateful event."

"Abram also studies the stars and watches for Sirius to lead Amon Re." After a pause Sarai continued, "I wish rivers like the Nile crossed all deserts." Sarai pointed. "There's another pyramid."

Are pyramids made for eternal life? Hagar wondered as they sailed past. *If so, why do they speak in silence?*

It seemed as if Sarai had heard her thoughts when she said, "Pyramids are prayers in stone, but they speak only of loneliness and sadness."

"We come from darkness and live in Amon Re's light and then return to blackness," Sit-Hathor-Yunet added. "Death seems so final but the pyramids assure eternal life. It's all a mystery."

"But El Shaddai has drawn the veil from the face of death for us," Sarai commented.

"Do you really believe one God can be all wise?" Pharaoh's sister questioned.

"Yes. Because He made the world He knows everything. He hears us speak, and He knows even our thoughts. We can't hide from Him."

"Egypt trembles before many gods," Sit-Hathor-Yunet replied. "But Amon Re is hot and the boats are stopping until it's cooler."

After the flotilla of royal boats resumed its journey Sarai asked Hagar if she could play the girl's harp. Surprised, Hagar handed it to her and said, "Play and sing." She sensed Sarai's skill as the woman tuned the harp.

"Sing to us of Ur of the Chaldees," Sit-Hathor-Yunet urged.

"The Nile reminds me of some Sumerian water songs," Sarai replied.

When Sarai finished the songs, eyes glowing with happiness, she asked, "Sit-Hathor-Yunet, would you like them in your language?"

"Yes, teach me the songs."

"Here's one Sumerians sang when the Tigris River didn't rise.

" 'Famine was severe,
   Nothing was produced.
   At the small rivers
   There was no "washing of the hands."
   The waters rose not high,
   The fields are not watered.
   There was no digging of ditches;
   In all the lands there was no vegetation.
   Only weeds grew.' "

"Then water came," Sarai said and continued singing.

" 'The high waters poured over the fields.
   Behold now, everything on earth
   Rejoiced afar at the king of the land.
   The fields produced abundant grain,
   The vineyard and orchard bore their fruit,
   The harvest was heaped up in granaries and hills.
   The Lord made mourning to disappear from the land.'

"Now I'll sing one about Dumuzi, a Sumerian ruler. It reminds me of our experience in Canaan when there was no rain." Sarai closed her eyes and deep emotion filled her voice:

" 'Hot belching winds blew,
   Grass knotted and scorched its roots,
   Olives hardened and fell to the ground.
   Flocks and herds melted before our eyes.
   Brittle leaves of weeds rattled.
   Crops were stillborn in the womb of nature.
   The cup from the peg has fallen,
   The shepherd's crook has vanished,
   A falcon holds a lamb in its claws,
   Young goats drag their beards in the dust.

Sheep of the fold paw the ground with bent limbs.
The churn lies shattered, no milk is poured;
The sheepfold is given over to the wind.' "

As Sarai sang Hagar sensed that the Sand-dweller woman longed
to be in Canaan again. She also heard Sit-Hathor-Yunet say, "Teach
those songs to me in Sumerian." The rest of the afternoon the two
princesses taught each other songs of their heritage.

After four days the boats docked at Abydos, the city with a sanc-
tity possessed by no other place in Egypt. Amidst great confusion
they settled into the Royal Inn. Later on the veranda Hagar said to
Kheti, "I wish the festival could start right now." The girl sighed.
"Tomorrow, day 12 of the month, we'll at last see with our eyes the
Mystery Festivals."

Next morning Hagar blinked in astonishment at the throngs of
people filling the streets. The air buzzed with talk and laughter. She
pressed closer to Sarai and Sit-Hathor-Yunet as the two women rode
along in their carrying chairs. Soon priests clad in sacred vestments
appeared, followed by musicians, singers, and dancers. The musicians sang of the north wind, the Nile flood, and celestial waters.
Hagar's pulse throbbed with the music and she felt an intense desire
to sing with them. Her chance came when the crowd burst into a
song that linked Osiris, the symbol of vegetation, to the waxing and
waning moon. Then a priest's eulogy of Osiris, the dying and resur-
recting god, stirred the girl to tears.

On day 14 teams of long-horned African cows, decked in color-
ful trappings, pulled gold-colored plows. Earlier the Nile flood had
deposited silt over the dried, cracked earth. Now the plowshares
tore open silt-filled crevices. Sowers, hands and faces painted green,
followed the plow, scattering seed. Herds of decorated goats led by
stumbling and staggering servants came next. As the animals' hooves
tramped in the seed, it symbolized that Osiris, as planted seed,
would spring forth into new life.

While it was still dark the morning of day 16, the first day of the
main Mystery Festival, Kheti whispered, "Hagar, will we now understand death and eternity?"

"Set your heart on it. We'll understand."

"I'm afraid to die. Just the thought of it gives me a lonesome feeling."

Hagar picked up a lamp and stared at its little flame. "I don't want to wander in the unknown either."

The girls joined their mistresses and headed for the temple courts. In the distance shadowy figures with their own lamps hurried toward the temple. Throngs crowded the great court. Everyone grew quiet when torches appeared and trumpets sounded. Fear mingled with expectancy in Hagar's heart.

The Chief Seal-bearer, Ikhernofret the revered, stood near the temple and lifted his clear voice. "His Majesty Sen Wosret directed me to Abydos to adorn the secret image of Osiris with fine gold from Nubia. I decked the breast of the lord of Abydos with lapis lazuli and turquoise, fine gold and all costly stones, ornaments of a god's body. I was pure of hand in decking the god. I am a priest whose fingers are clean. His Majesty chose me to direct the Mystery Festival."

Then a priest named Sehetep-ib-re took his position before the temple. As he chanted with great authority the familiar story of Osiris, other priests pantomimed it.

"Osiris, free from evil, was once a king in the form of man on earth! His jealous brother murdered him, but his sister-wife, Isis, searched until she found him. With the aid of priests she mummified his body. The god Thoth and a serpent-headed goddess intervened. With their help Osiris was able to bring about his own resurrection. He then climbed up the ladder to heaven where the gods made him ruler over the nether world and judge of the dead."

Afterward, musicians and dancers led a procession. Some carried statues of former god-kings. Pharaoh Sen Wosret, richly adorned, followed in a thronelike palanquin carried by servants. Fan bearers and attendants with lamps and torches walked on each side. At his appearance people prostrated themselves before their god-king.

Next priests carrying 34 papyrus boats followed. In them burned 365 lamps that had been lit by sacred fire. The fragrance of incense carried prayers to Osiris. The first boat carried statues of the ram god of Mendes and Anubis, jackal god of the dead. The second held one of Isis, wife of Osiris. Thirty-two other gods followed, each in a lighted boat.

At dawn a priest placed a funeral bier before the temple. Two virgins portraying Osiris's sisters, Nephthys and Isis, stood at the head and foot. Priests bore the mummy image of Osiris out of the temple, placed it on the bier, and lifted it to their shoulders. Nephthys led them while Isis followed the bier, uttering piercing shrieks and lamentations.

Caught up in the emotion of the ceremony, Hagar began to cry as she, with the royal household, joined the weeping and wailing procession. Worshipers with shaved heads beat their breasts. Others inflicted wounds on their bodies in imitation of the mutilated body of Osiris.

A mile and a half to the southwest the procession stopped for the burial in Peqer. A mountain of votive offering jars, placed there by pilgrims commemorating the life, death, and resurrection of Osiris, buried the tomb. It had been the ancient tomb of Zer, a first dynasty pharaoh. After a few minutes of silence, the priests, chanting a mournful melody, committed Osiris to the tomb. As they placed the image in the tomb the people became wild with grief. Tears and sobs turned into wails and shrieks of agony, and then lapsed into sobs as singers proclaimed the greatness of Osiris.

Hagar knew that people from all over Egypt sent their bodies to be buried in this cemetery. Royal officials, government emissaries, and even common people visiting Abydos would erect a tablet in the cemetery begging Osiris for eternity. They left plaques both for themselves and for relatives. Mummies of pharaohs and nobles often rested for a time beside Osiris before being placed in their permanent tombs. Their visit in the Abydos temple ensured them favor in the judgment. Hagar vowed to place a plaque for herself there someday. She hoped the festival impressed Sarai.

Day after day Hagar watched various pageants depict incidents in the life of Osiris. "I wish I could live in Abydos forever," she told Kheti. Between the pageants they attended tournaments and banquets in honor of Osiris. Crowds from neighboring villages swelled the throng and some became loud and noisy from too much beer.

On the last day Sit-Hathor-Yunet's entourage again went to the temple court. After the musicians, singers, and dancers performed, a procession from Peqer arrived bearing a bier on which lay a statue of Osiris, draped as a mummy and wearing a white crown. Nephthys and Isis again stood at each end. A priest wearing a hawk's head mask and representing Horus stood behind the bier. Two other priests, one wearing a jackal head and the other a frog head, stood on each side of Horus. Above the image hung a figure of a hawk, its gold wings reflecting the light of Amon Re. Under the bier were two snake goddesses, one called Her-tept.

Hagar watched for the key element in the festival, Osiris pulling himself to his knees. As the crowd held its breath she saw Osiris, holding his scepter and flail, slowly rise. His resurrection accomplished, the priests carried the image to the temple. Freed from his mummy wrappings, Osiris came out to the ladder made of knotted thongs. With the help of the priests he made his way to the top of the temple. There more priests received him as Osiris symbolically stepped from the ladder into the afterworld and received the right to rule its inhabitants.

Each day, the people believed, the Ba of Osiris would secretly descend as a hawk and behold his temple. Daily he installed himself upon his image. Hagar wondered if the belief was true.

Osiris's followers taught that he had attained his exalted position because he had lived a sinless life. The most remarkable thing about him was that his body had never decayed like those of ordinary human beings.

As the last and most important pageant approached, Hagar, now near exhaustion, saw everywhere the emotion-ravaged faces of the other pilgrims. Their concern was for life after death. At the final ritual every eye focused on Apis, a black bull decorated with gold. A priest proclaimed, "Oh people of the Two Lands, behold your god, Apis, living image of Osiris. Apis, the Bull of Heaven, is the son of Osiris as well as of Ptah." The crowd drank in each word.

"There is a white triangle on his forehead and a figure of a hawk, the soul of Osiris on his back," the priest continued. "A beetle is on his tongue with magic words written on it for the judgment. The scarab beetles roll mud and ox-dung into spheres like Amon Re. They roll the balls to the edge of the desert. Soon a new generation of beetles appears. To us they symbolize resurrection and life. They help our dead enter eternity." As he finished a sigh escaped from the crowd.

Nine virgin singers chanted hymns to Osiris while dancers formed a circle around Apis to act out the story of Osiris. The hymns extolled Osiris as lord of ma'at (truth) and as prince of eternity. It seemed to Hagar that some of the ideas presented contradicted each other, but she couldn't sort them out.

Finally Apis, the dancers, and the musicians disappeared. Then the priests placed Osiris on a throne with nine stairsteps leading to it. Anubis, an attendant of Osiris, presided over the balance that would weigh the heart against the feather of ma'at (truth and cosmic order) in the judgment of the dead. Thoth, as scribe, was ready to record the verdicts. All the gods and goddesses of the senses were present. Amemait, the devourer, a monster with the head and jaws of a crocodile, waited off to the side. A tribunal of 42 assistant judges were also present.

Thus the judgment began before a tired and watchful audience. Singers introduced the scene with a song that Hagar knew and liked.

"Lo, he has come as Orion;
Lo, Osiris has come as Orion,
Conceived of sky, born of dusk.
Sky conceived you and Orion,
Dusk gave birth to you and Orion.
Who lives by the god's command?
You shall live!
You shall rise with Orion in the eastern sky,
You shall sit with Orion in the western sky,
Your third is Sirius, pure of thrones,
She is your guide on the sky's good paths,
In the Field of Rushes."

Hagar sighed. The song raised many unanswered questions. It reminded her of the ancient belief that Orion and Sirius were the homes of a departed Ba. While the music continued, Hagar studied the steady gaze of Osiris on his throne. So he controlled death, the major issue that governed the actions of the Egyptian people. What did it all mean? Why was eternity dependent on the character of one's life on earth? But then a person could obtain exemptions from the penalties in the hereafter. Why should she fear? She turned back to the line of priests representing souls facing eternal judgment.

In the judgment pageant the first soul addressed in turn, each of the 42 judges. Each judged one of 42 sins. The priest representing the soul first pleaded not guilty of stealing, then passed to the next judge and pleaded not guilty of murder. And so it went until the gods had judged all sins such as lying, robbing minors, deceit, false witness, reviling, eavesdropping, sexual impurity, adultery, and trespasses against the gods or against the dead. Anubis weighed the deceased's heart on a balance with the feather of ma'at while Thoth recorded the verdicts. Then the defendant stood before Osiris who studied his record in silence.

At last Osiris spoke. "I condemn your preserved body to hunger and thirst in the heavy darkness of death. Eternal sleeping will be your occupation. Your Ba belongs to the devourer. Your name will be taken away and your identity lost." Hagar felt his words reach down her throat and pull her heart out.

The expression on the faces of the onlookers was no longer exhaustion but terror. Heartbroken wails filled Hagar's ears and she shuddered. The victim's final destiny still remained a mysterious secret. This was the second death her people feared most and sought with all their power to avoid.

Another being now stood before Osiris. After reading Thoth's record, he said to the soul, "Your spirit is indestructible. You shall live because Osiris lives. Eternity is before you. A messenger will take you to well-watered fields. You will be a celestial star."

Cheers thundered from thousands of throats. The priest-soul held a scarab so the audience could see it. The people understood the defendant had employed magic to sway the judgments. On the scarab were inscribed the magic words, "O heart rise not up against me as a witness." When a guilty one stood before Osiris the scarab with its powerful words silenced the voices of hearts and tongues. The scarab hid the evil of the defendant's heart.

One of the most sacred ceremonies of the great festival followed the judgment scene. It consisted of raising to an upright position

Osiris's Column of Tet in front of the temple. From the top down it showed the plumes, horns, disk breastplate and pectoral of the god. When the Tet was in place the great Mystery Festival came to an end.

The crowd immediately swarmed around the priests, buying scarabs to escape the penalties of their own judgment. But the priests turned away those who did not have enough to purchase a scarab. Both frightened and furious at the attitude of the religious leaders, Hagar wondered if the priests were only interested in increasing their wealth.

Sit-Hathor-Yunet and Sarai ordered their servants to carry them back to the Inn. Their attendants followed in silence. It seemed to Hagar that all human beings were eternal travelers with their destinies still shrouded in mystery. The spiritual world seemed to her still an unknown, mysterious, and forbidding place.

Exile

口口口口口口口口口口口口口口口口口口口口口口口口口口口口口口口口

Hagar, I see no sign of Sen Wosret," Kheti said, pointing toward the royal vessel as they waited to board it.

Squinting, Hagar searched the faces on the boat. "I see priest Ameni and scribe Itruri but not Pharaoh."

"His Majesty earlier sailed upriver to Dendera and Philae to inspect temples," Sit-Hathor-Yunet explained to Sarai. "He should already be at the palace by now."

The girls slapped mosquitoes as they watched the flotilla of skiffs begin to drift down river. Hagar handed Kheti a palm reed basket. "Put this in the boat for Sarai."

When ready, they cast off. Boat followed boat past the fishing craft along the shore. Quietness settled over them. Now relaxed, Hagar inhaled the fresh north wind and watched the Nile flow ahead into the distance. Amon Re promised a perfect day.

"Eeeeeeooooow!"

Like lightning word passed from boat to boat that a melapeterius had grazed a fisherman dangling his leg in the river. The eel-like fish delivered a powerful shock, which caused the victim to tremble then stiffen.

"Will he be all right?" Sarai asked.

"He'll recover," an oarsman explained. "Now most of the noise you hear comes from netting moonfish. They're covered with spikes and puff up into big balls. When taken from the water they go flat with a loud noise."

"The peasants dry them in the sun," Sit-Hathor-Yunet added.

When conversation lagged Hagar thought again of the events of the Mystery Festival and remembered paying Sarai little attention beyond that required by her duties while in Abydos.

Something Sit-Hathor-Yunet said caught her attention. "Even after a day of rest I'm exhausted. Sarai, even at your age you don't look tired."

"My strength increased as I walked the hills of Canaan. We're outdoors much of the time."

"His Majesty's heart melts at the sight of your strength, beauty, and wisdom. You speak new words, new thoughts. Both Pharaoh and I want you in the palace."

"Sit-Hathor-Yunet, you're my friend but I can't stay. El Shaddai wants me in Abram's camp."

"We can include El Shaddai with our gods. Then He'd belong to a powerful nation."

Hagar watched Sarai carefully as the woman responded. "El Shaddai already belongs to the whole world. He should not share worship with other gods." The girl noticed the oarsmen, servants, and attendants intently listening to the conversation.

"If you worship just one god," Sit-Hathor-Yunet asked, "how can you be sure he's the right one? Why not be safe and worship them all?"

"You have gods for each hour, each day, each month, and each season plus hundreds of others. Can you possibly worship them all?"

Hagar squirmed. She wanted to answer herself but forced herself to just listen as Sit-Hathor-Yunet replied, "We give more worship to the most powerful gods such as Osiris and Amon Re. At the Mystery Festival you saw the splendor of Osiris. Did it not impress you?"

Apparently choosing her words with great care, Sarai said, "My heart ached for the crowds who, seeking eternity, bought scarabs from priests for protection in the judgment. I wished they knew El Shaddai who knows everything and can give eternal life."

"But Osiris can bestow everlasting life."

"Only a Creator God can do that. The priests at the festival taught that eternity can be secured without right choices. Sit-Hathor-Yunet, Osiris was fooled. If priests can so easily deceive him with words on scarabs, can he truly be wise?"

Sarai's words raised still more questions in Hagar's heart.

Sit-Hathor-Yunet's glance swept over the servants and attendants then back to Sarai before she answered. "The priests selling scarabs made me uneasy," she said cautiously.

"May I tell you what I learned while I have traveled through many lands?"

Pharaoh's sister nodded.

"Abram's people traveled from Ur to Haran to Canaan to your land. In our journey we have discovered that people have become the slaves of thousands of other gods."

At this Sit Hathor-Yunet leaned toward Sarai. "You make my heart uneasy. Are you saying that something is wrong with our gods?"

Sympathy was plain in Sarai's voice. "Yes, there are impostors who use magic and other mysterious powers to deceive us."

Pharaoh's sister stared at her for a long time. Hagar began to fear the woman was angry. Then Sit-Hathor-Yunet whispered rapidly, "Tell me more."

Sarai's voice grew in power as she talked. Hagar had already heard the story in the household of the women, but its repetition stimulated new thoughts. She again felt dismay over the choice of Ish and Ishshah that broke the heart of the world. "Since the evil one—you call him Apophis—used the serpent to say to Ishshah, 'You shall not die,' why do you have serpent-headed gods?"

Pharaoh's sister looked startled. "I don't know."

"Why did a serpent-headed god help Osiris gain life in the resurrection pageant?"

"Our ancestors taught that serpents know how to prevent the second death and bestow eternal life. The priests understand this, but to me it's a mystery," Sit-Hathor-Yunet admitted.

"Some believe the evil one's words, 'You shall not die,' because they do not want to return to clay. No serpent-headed god can make the words of Apophis true. However, El Shaddai has promised to send a Redeemer who will forgive wrong choices and give eternal life. While He's not here now, He will come in the future."

"You must have in mind Osiris. He has already lived as a man. And even Sen Wosret was born of the god, Amon Re."

"No, not Osiris. El Shaddai told Abram that the Redeemer is yet to come."

"Why would He tell Abram and not our priests?"

"But He has told priests and prophets. For example, He told Melchizedek, a prophet and king, who lived near us in Canaan."

Sit-Hather-Yunet sat in silence for a long time. "Sarai," she said finally, "you are skilled of tongue but you tangle my thoughts. Help me to understand."

Everyone in the boat listened with interest to Sarai. Hagar discovered that the foundation and structure of life was the power of choice guided by El Shaddai's laws. She learned that wrong choices had led to a world of error, making it hard to sort out truth. Error wrapped in truth could be powerful. Sarai explained that people often blamed El Shaddai for the trouble that followed their own wrong choices. They failed to recognize that such choices have within themselves the seeds of destruction. Some sprouted rapidly while others were slow and might take years to germinate. A choice affected both the one making it and others as well. The Sand-dweller's next words seized Hagar's attention. "If error were removed from some hearts they'd shrivel up for they don't know any truth to fill the void.

"Little by little, century after century, the knowledge of El Shaddai has become lost," Sarai explained. "For this reason He has prophets to whom He speaks to keep truth from becoming extinct. El Shaddai says the descendants of a man now living will see the fulfillment of His promise to make a great nation of him. They will preserve His law and bring blessing to all the world."

Sarai paused to study her astonished audience. "You believe in Ptah, perhaps your name for El Shaddai, who is self-existent and immortal. Thus you know of this God who created all things but your priests have divided Him into hundreds of different gods."

When Sarai finished Hagar and the others released a deep sigh. After several minutes of silence Sit-Hathor-Yunet said, "Your thoughts are so vast I can hardly get my heart around them. I must carry them to Sen Wosret."

They soon docked. Although travel-weary, Hagar knew that she must learn more about Sarai's invisible God. Before she fell asleep that night she watched shafts of moonlight penetrate the room through the tiny window and remembered that the moon itself was a creation of El Shaddai.

"Hagar, Hagar, wake up." Sleepy as she was she still recognized Sarai's voice.

"What's wrong?" Raising herself up on one elbow, she stared into the dimness.

"There's great sickness in the palace. Come, bring a lamp. They say people are dying."

The girl jumped to her feet. "Has Maraket sent the royal physicians."

"Yes, but I want to help. Sit-Hathor-Yunet dispatched a messenger."

In the palace, lit by the flickering light of oil lamps and torches, they encountered confusion and anguished wailing. Priests, physicians, and servants hastened here and there while the rest of the household stood by helpless. Hagar followed Sarai into a room in which several young princes were vomiting, choking, and groaning. Their heads ached and they alternately flushed from fever and shivered from cold. Servants cleaned up each mess while Sarai wiped the fevered brow of the crown prince, Amenenhet, with a damp cloth. Hagar followed Sarai's example and tended another child. She glanced up to see a priest glaring at Sarai. Oblivious to the priest's reaction, Sarai went from room to room caring for the sick, much to the surprise of the servants.

Suddenly a messenger approached, bowed, and said to Sarai, "His Majesty Sen Wosret wishes to see you. Come." As they followed him they met Ameni leaving Pharaoh's quarters. He passed them with a fierce scowl, a reaction that Hagar interpreted as indicating trouble. Inside they found the agitated ruler pacing the floor. He stopped as the messenger approached. "Great Majesty, son of Amon Re and ruler of the Two Lands, I present Princess Sarai."

The Sand-dweller woman did not wait to be addressed. "Your majesty, I'm sorry sickness has stricken the palace. I'll help where I can."

"You?" Pharaoh stormed, his face red with anger. "The priests say your God has sent a plague on the palace. Why?"

"I do not understand."

"You say El Shaddai doesn't want you to marry me."

"That is true."

Pharaoh yelled to his attendant, "Bring my counselors." Then he turned back to her. "Tell me why your God doesn't want you to marry me," he demanded, his knuckles white in his clenched fists. For an instant he seemed to lose himself, and Hagar noticed his body shake.

"You already have many beautiful women in your household," Sarai said hesitatingly.

Pharaoh reddened as he sneered, "Your God desires you to be the only one?"

She studied him a moment, then in a quiet voice said, "I'm already married."

"Married?" Sen Wosret roared. "What is this?"

Sleepy, half-dressed counselors arrived, but became wide awake as Sarai in a strong voice said, "Yes, Abram is my husband."

Astonished, Hagar and others gasped and saw rage race over Pharaoh's face. He turned to his attendant. "Have Abram here tomorrow. For now I'll meet with the counselors." Again he faced Sarai, "When Abram arrives I'll send for you." He gestured in dismissal. "Go back to the household of women." He turned his back to them and they followed the attendant out of the royal chambers and walked in silence back to the women's quarters.

The next morning messengers reported that the health of the princes had improved. That afternoon Pharaoh's attendant came for Sarai. She and Hagar followed him to Sen Wosret's council chamber. Government officials, priests, and scribes huddled in clusters. Abram and Eliezer waited off by themselves. Sarai followed the attendant to one side. While Ameni took his place with the priests, Hagar saw Abram glance at Sarai. Pharaoh, his displeasure evident, entered with his entourage who escorted him to his throne. When seated the monarch let silence reign while he studied the uneasiness in the room.

Looking directly at Abram, he thundered, "Stand before me." Abram and Eliezer approached Sen Wosret. Hagar trembled at her father's angry words. "I, Sen Wosret, ruler of the Two Lands, have been kind to you." He jumped to his feet and pointed at Abram. "In return you've brought sorrow on this palace, a crime worthy of death." Pharaoh paused to determine the effect of his words.

Hagar froze with fear for Sarai and Abram. However, she detected no nervousness in Abram as he faced the king. After a long silence Pharaoh demanded, "Why did you call Sarai your sister?"

"Your Majesty, Sarai is my sister, the daughter of my father but not my mother," the Sand-dweller replied firmly.

"And she is also your wife?"

"Yes."

"Why did you conceal this relationship?"

Abram lifted his hands. "Because it is rumored Egyptians kill husbands to steal their wives."

"My servants negotiated for your sister in good faith."

The Sand-dweller sighed. "Never did I guess she would come to the attention of Pharaoh."

The man's answer seemed to calm the Egyptian ruler, but he still said bitterly, "Your half-truth has become a whole lie."

"Your Majesty, I beg your forgiveness," Abram said, bowing. "If I find favor in your sight, restore my wife. I'll return your bride price."

Hagar's thoughts raced. She couldn't stand the idea of Sarai leaving the household of the women. As she watched Pharaoh seemed to relax. He glanced at Sarai and back at Abram. "My sister says your invisible God is extremely powerful. He honors you by His intervention. So that El Shaddai's wrath will not continue against my kingdom, keep the bride price and leave the Two Lands."

Ameni stepped forward. "But Your Highness, the bride price should come to the temple." Sen Wosret waved him away.

"Your Majesty is kind," Abram said, bowing again. "We'll return to Canaan."

Pharaoh glanced at Ameni then in a firm but kind voice said to Abram, "So your God will be satisfied, I'll send more servants and cattle with you. For your protection an armed guard will escort you to the border."

The sorrow in Hagar's heart exploded into agony. She was going to lose Sarai and her chance to learn more about El Shaddai. From the first day the girl's heart had knit to Sarai's as though she had known her forever. She saw Pharaoh turn to Sarai with sadness in his eyes. "My sister loves you, but you may go with your husband in peace."

Suddenly Hagar knew that she must do something and forced herself to speak. Her distressed voice carried through the chamber while astonished eyes turned to her. "Your Majesty, you favor Abram and are kind to Sarai. I beg to go with Sarai to Canaan."

"What?" Pharaoh exclaimed. "You will be no more than a servant there with her."

Sarai stepped forward. "A handmaid perhaps, but Hagar and I have become friends. With your permission she is welcome with us. May I also tell you that I'm sorry for the trouble our presence in Egypt has caused you."

Pharaoh looked long at her. "The palace will miss you," he said finally. Then turning to Abram, he said, "I place the future support of my daughter in your hands."

Leaving Egypt

▢▢▢▢▢▢▢▢▢▢▢▢▢▢▢▢▢▢▢▢▢▢▢▢▢▢▢▢▢▢▢▢

As Hagar rode along the edge of the desolate red land loneliness threatened to overwhelm her. The swinging motion of her perch on the camel twisted her stomach into knots and the caravan dust choked her.

When she had told Sarai that she wanted to go with her, it had been both the easiest and hardest thing she had ever said. She regarded the house of the women as a prison and wanted to leave it forever. Yet the chance to leave both thrilled and frightened her. Now it frightened her to abandon her familiar life.

With tears Kheti and she vanished from each other's life. Hagar had transferred all her bonds of affection to El Shaddai and Sarai. She tried to convince herself that ties of blood couldn't compare in strength with those of the heart.

Now Hagar brushed at her dusty clothes. Packed were the enameled collars, the armbands and necklaces of gold. Her face became grimy with dust and her hair was dirty and matted. As she squinted at the sun-bleached landscape, she thought, *I'm leaving to live among Sand-dwellers. Will I come back to die and be embalmed like Sinuhe? I don't want my body to crumble, causing me to perish the second death.*

She stared into the distance behind her where she could still see the dark line of the Nile. *I'll always remember the palms creating walls of green against the sky and tiny villages like muddy footprints in green fields.* She sat straighter on the camel and wondered about the Khamsin wind. It blew desert dust from the southwest. At first gentle, it would later pound and whip the Two Lands with fine desert sand. Lasting some 50 days, the Khamsin wind blasted sand and fine dust through every crack. Sand-filled food crunched when chewed and clothes carried a film of dust. It blew into ears, eyes, and skin until sand and people seemed one. Concerned, Hagar thought, *It's too early. We'll be away from the Two Lands before the wind comes.*

Far ahead she saw the leaders of the caravan and Pharaoh's escort. The shouts of the drivers, children's laughter, and the complaints of animals mingled into a confusing roar of sound. Hagar decided that Sarai was right—Abram must have a thousand people, and Pharaoh had sent numerous guards as an escort. The caravan made its way through golden barley grass bending before the breeze.

Amon Re descended toward the pyramids. The pharaohs of the Old Kingdom were now only faded memories, reminding her how ancient her people were. *I'm leaving the eternal home of my ancestors,* she thought. *I must remember them forever.*

The caravan shifted northeast, still following the boundary between vegetation and desert, letting distance swallow the pyramids. Then, as Amon Re neared the horizon, the caravan stopped at a caravansary. A servant tapped the knees of her camel and its legs folded underneath its body, lowering Hagar so that she could climb down off the animal. Once she was on the ground her own legs wobbled. "Hagar, did you like your camel ride?" Sarai asked as she approached.

"I'd rather walk or ride a donkey tomorrow. I ache all over."

"It'll get easier," Sarai promised. "We'll rest for a few days at Tharu on the border. There we'll buy supplies to cross the desert. After six days work we have a day of rest to worship El Shaddai." She began giving orders to servants, when a startled Egyptian voice shouted, "Hagar!"

The girl turned. "Khuni!" she yelled.

"Why are you here?" they both asked at the same time.

"I'm attending Sarai. Pharaoh gave his consent. But you?"

The boy's happiness shone from his face like the rays of Amon Re. "I'm working for Abram. My wages are black donkeys from Damascus. They carry twice as much as gray ones. Soon I'll be a merchant."

"Khuni, I'm glad you're here. I've been lonely."

"There's another Egyptian girl in the caravan. Her name is Meret.

75

You'll like her—she's with her family."

"I must find her, but first I need to help Sarai. We'll talk later."

The boy nodded. "And I must find out where the sheep will stay tonight."

Early the next day Abram, some servants, and a few of Pharaoh's guards left on fast camels for Bubastis to buy copper and bronze weapons and tools as well as papyrus scrolls and ink. They would rejoin the main caravan before nightfall.

The rest of the day Hagar alternately walked and rode a donkey. Travel wasn't burdensome for Abram had told Pharaoh's guards that they would travel slowly because of the children and the young of the flocks and herds.

Hagar concentrated on the language of the Sand-dwellers and the ease with which she learned it surprised her. She was happy that Khuni was here but she especially wanted to talk Egyptian with the girl Meret.

Before they reached the border Abram returned from Bubastis and edged the caravan east of Tharu, a garrison town sprawled on a hill. The feeling of impending separation from Egypt that it symbolized now numbed Hagar.

Near a fire pit, built by a previous caravan, Abram's servants pitched his goat-hair tent and erected a stone alter. The rest of the tents formed two rough circles around Abram's.

"Hagar," Sarai called from the inner circle. "Come here. This is your tent next to mine so you'll be near when I need you."

The girl stared at the mats the servants were arranging on the dirt floor. Disbelief filled her voice. "This is your home?"

"Yes, for 15 days until the full moon. Abram will shear sheep. He'll trade wool for supplies for the journey." Sarai paused for a few moments, then continued, "Things will be more comfortable at Bethel. Here are the donkeys. Let's help unpack our things."

"All right, Mistress," the girl said stiffly.

"Hagar."

"Yes?" She glanced at Sarai.

"In Abram's camp all are equal before El Shaddai. We speak to each other as family and friends."

"I'll remember," she said as each turned to the task of settling their respective tents.

Later she watched Abram slay a lamb and burn it on the pillar of stones. Then he lifted his hands high and talked to El Shaddai.

When darkness fell Hagar sat alone at the door of her tent. As she hugged her knees she realized how much she missed Kheti. Stars crowded the sky and the campfires smoldered, tinging the air with smoke. Hagar listened to the murmur of voices, the whimper of children, and the occasional bark of a scavenging dog. When a chill fell over the camp, Hagar rose, went into her tent, and dropped the flap. Before she fell asleep she heard the wail of a jackal.

At dawn Pharaoh's guards, now friends of Abram, returned from Tharu. Abram served them a breakfast of barley bread, olives, cheese, and figs. Afterward they bid the camp a noisy farewell.

Several women with servants came to Sarai's tent. They led donkeys with baskets tied on their back and hanging from their sides. Sarai motioned to Hagar. "Come, we're going to Tharu. Pharaoh's guards reported several traders caravans there. I'll need you."

The girl hastened into her tent and returned with a bag.

When they rode into Tharu, Sarai said, "Just smell this trading post and listen to the uproar." Merchants and buyers clustered under awnings of rough cloth or branches. Hagar glanced into stalls filled with every conceivable thing. Smells of baking bread mixed with pungent animal odors. She watched Sarai, through her servants, barter for linen, more papyrus scrolls, sandals, garments, bone needles, and baskets.

When they paused at one stall a trader studied them. "You're Sarai, Abram's wife?"

"Yes. Are you from Canaan?"

"My name is Dothan. I've traded with Abram in Canaan."

"Has he ordered raisin cakes from you? These look good."

He ran his fingers through his beard. "Yes, I'm sending him a hundred donkey loads. He's to give me wool."

"He's shearing all the sheep before we cross the desert."

Dothan nodded. "A wise man, your husband. May he trade all his wool before he enters the desert."

From a stall nearby they heard a cold contemptuous voice spit out, "Go away—leave." Hagar edged closer to see what was going on.

"Give it to me."

"No, that's final." A man emerged, hastening down the street.

"They squabble over prices," Sarai told her. "It often happens, but look there's a merchant tossing dates to children."

Soon the baskets on the donkeys were full, but before they left Hagar let Merke, an Egyptian, help her trade some small pieces of jewelry for boots. "They'll make walking comfortable," she explained to Sarai.

"You trade well. They'll also protect against scorpions. Now let's leave this confusion and get back to camp."

As the days passed they packed the supplies obtained at Tharu. Each night they gathered at the fire pit. One afternoon Hagar noticed a tall shy girl speaking to what must be her parents in Egyptian. All through the evening sacrifice, the songs, and stories, she stole glances at the girl. Hagar knew that she also watched her. Later Hagar went to her and asked in Egyptian, "Are you Meret?"

"Yes. And you must be Hagar."

"I am. Khuni told me about you. Your family is with you?"

"Yes. They have accepted El Shaddai as their God."

"Is that why you are here?"

"We are weavers, and we'll be retainers in Abram's household."

"It's good to speak Egyptian again. Do you speak the Sanddweller's tongue?"

"I am learning. But come to our tent and converse in our tongue."

"I will soon." Hagar started to leave, then paused. "Is Khuni staying with the shepherds?"

"No, he and my father, with a few shepherds, went to the Sea of Reeds to fish. They'll sundry them to use as we cross the desert."

"When did they leave?"

"As soon as we pitched camp. Abram asked them to be back three days before we leave here."

"Abram hopes to leave in six days," Hagar said. "Come to my tent soon. It's next to Sarai's."

While the caravan waited for the fishing party to return, Hagar continued to help Sarai pack. "At En-mishpat we'll rest and repack to go north to Bethel," Sarai told her.

The girl picked up some squares of cloth. "These aren't clothes."

"Pack them with the clothes, anyway. They're to keep off sun and sand."

"How about food?"

"The women are grinding flour so we'll not have to carry any grinding stones. Eliezer and his men are packing it. We'll stow the lamps, oil, extra boots, and black kohl. We want to make sure we have enough khol to protect our eyes from the desert sun."

The girl watched her for a moment as she worked, then said, "Sarai, you know so much."

The woman acknowledged the compliment with a smile. "I've lived long. You'll know more when you're older."

"I like being your attendant, but I wish you were my mother."

Sarai's smile widened and her eyes sparkled. "Thank you, Hagar. I look forward to being a mother. El Shaddai has promised Abram a son. I hope it happens soon."

"A baby? Oh, Sarai, may I care for him?"

She nodded, then glanced off into the distance behind the girl. "Look, Hagar, the fishing party has returned."

Hagar stared toward Meret's tent on the far side of the encampment where she saw Khuni unloading the donkeys. When he finished he approached them.

"Shalom, Sarai," Khuni said in Canaanite, then greeted Hagar in Egyptian.

"Did you catch enough fish for the whole camp?" Sarai asked.

"We caught thousands—enough to feed the whole camp—just on the first day." Then he faced Hagar. "I know you like curious things. You should have seen the fish carrying lamps in the Sea of Reeds."

The girl laughed. "How can fish carry lamps?"

"Hagar, it's true. Under each eye they have a little lamp. They can blink it on and off. We saw them shining in the sea at night."

She clapped her hands. "I want to see them. Did you bring some back?"

"No, they're little fellows, about as long as the width of a hand. One night we saw hundreds shining around our boat with a blue-green light. It was like floating with the stars."

"Why would fish have lights?" Hagar asked.

Khuni's voice had a ring of importance. "They're night fish, so they need light to find food."

Hagar sighed. "If I were a boy, life would be more fun."

He shrugged. "We start across the desert soon. Then you'll have all the adventure you'll ever want." Glancing at her bare feet, he added, "Wear boots."

That night Abram began instructing those who had never crossed the desert how to prepare for the journey. He used a square cloth to illustrate how they should protect themselves from the sun and wind-carried sand, and explained how to conserve water. "I've hired a desert guide to lead the caravan, so listen to what he tells you."

The last night after the special rest day a nearly full moon bathed the camp. "The trip will be difficult," Abram warned. "Stay with the caravan at all times. Remain within speaking distance to those in front and back of you. We'll start at dawn when it's cool, rest a short time when Amon Re is overhead, and travel in the evening by the full moon."

Across the Desert

Only half-awake and with her muscles aching, Hagar stumbled into the predawn light and tried to ease her morning hunger by drinking from her waterskin. A wave of loneliness swept over her, and tears filled her eyes. *What have I gotten into?* she thought. *It was never like this with Sarai in Egypt.*

She became aware of shadowy forms running back and forth like ants after someone had began digging in an anthill with a stick. Tents, including her own, came down with lightning speed. Donkeys brayed while the camels protested the bundles of household goods being secured over their humps. The cries of children, the shouts of the donkey boys, the commands of the herders, the bleating of sheep and goats, and the bawling of cattle shattered the desert silence. Out of the semidarkness Khuni emerged with several servants. "We've come to load your goods so that you can help Sarai."

"They're ready." She shoved a bundle toward him. "But why the hurry to leave the border of Egypt?"

He looked surprised. "Far places beckon. Remember when you told me that you wanted to travel?"

His matter-of-factness helped calm her. "Why should I fear. I'll set my heart like sun-dried clay!"

Khuni let the remark pass. Glancing at her bare feet, he firmly told her, "Dress for the desert. Wear a covering on your head and boots on your feet. And braid your hair to protect it against wind."

"Khuni, you're not my master," she laughed. But she pulled a pair of boots and a scarf from a basket. "This basket rides with me because it also has kohl to protect my eyes from Amon Re's light."

She dropped the boots into the basket and twirled the headpiece in front of her.

"Put them on now!"

"Yes, master," she teased. Picking up the boots, she walked swiftly toward Sarai's tent. There she found the woman surrounded by baggage and was pleased that she now understood the commands Sarai gave to the servants. "These supplies for Bethel, load on camels. Over here are food supplies for the desert—pack them on donkeys."

"Sarai, I'm here to help."

She glanced at the girl. "Are you hungry? We can eat soon."

"I'm starving."

As she waited for Sarai to bring some food Hagar watched the commotion on the edge of the camp caused by the herders. They loaded some donkeys with two lambs, one to a basket on either side. Shouting herders with their cattle and thousands of noisy sheep and goats joined the animal caravan. Young boys carrying slings and spears walked beside the animals to protect them. Soon clouds of dust announced their departure.

Sarai opened a small basket and held it toward her. "Please eat."

Hagar tasted the cucumber stuffed with barley and chipped mutton. Although pleasantly surprised by the taste, she still wanted to lay aside the meat. It repelled her because it represented her native sheep-headed god, Khnemu. She missed her usual fish and fowl, but with Sarai near ate the unfamiliar food. Bread, olives, and cheese finished the meal. The girl felt at ease and comfortable with Sarai and wanted to be with her the rest of her life.

Carefully and slowly Sarai said in the Canaanite tongue, "Help the servants pack the desert food."

As she did Sarai's bidding she saw Abram approach. He took in the preparations with a nod of approval. "Sarai, Eliezer has sent the flocks and herds ahead so the herders can care for the ewes and cows nursing their young and not exhaust them. Seti, the desert guide, will lead the caravan. We are about to start. Listen for the trumpet."

When its blast echoed across the desert, the caravan organized with incredible speed. Hagar fell into step with the jerk-sway motion of her donkey. Her pack donkeys and a driver followed along behind her. Ahead Sarai rode a camel led by a string of donkeys and more camels. Abram headed the caravan. To the south Hagar saw dust devils twirl in a light wind.

Hagar faced east. Like Sinuhe, she could be courageous for she knew that Khuni and Meret still linked her with the Two Lands. Except for animal sounds and creaking of baggage they rode in silence toward the rising Amon Re. Hagar marveled at the trees bent by their constant struggle against the east winds that combed their branches back toward Egypt. She smiled at the lizards perched on rocks, waiting for Amen Re to warm them enough to begin their search for food.

Overhead Amon Re gathered strength as they rode deeper into the boundless desert. The expanse of rock and sand stretched eastward to the horizon. The tread of the camel on sand accompanied the muffled thud of donkey hoofs. The immensity of the desert made her feel empty and insignificant. Then her resolve to follow Sarai and El Shaddai flashed into her heart. With a renewed determination she studied the desolate landscape sweeping into the distance. At first it stretched away motionless and monotonous, but soon she saw unsuspected and surprising beauty. Small dusty gray lizards stood erect and other creatures slithered and scurried across the rocks and sand. Her spirits lifted. *Oh,* she breathed, *it is both the ugliest place in the world and the most beautiful. I hate every moment in this caravan but I wouldn't be anywhere else.*

Hagar, suddenly conscious of the swaying shapes ahead loaded with water skins, drank from her own supply. "I wonder if I was ever really thirsty before?" she asked her donkey. The morning breeze had stopped and Amon Re sailed high in the sky. She sweltered in the hot desert air. Shouts of "A mirage! A mirage!" halted the caravan. Hagar followed the pointing fingers to the horizon where she saw a grove of date palms around a lake.

A voice yelled, "We're near water."

"It's not real," muttered a nearby donkey driver.

Seti, the guide, rode back along the caravan. He was thin as though Amon Re had burned away his flesh. His camel knelt and he unraveled his legs from the baggage. "Get off your animals," he ordered. "Lie down on the sand and look at the water." Hagar dismounted to the hot sand, rolled over on her stomach, and stared. The lake came within a few cubits of her, then receded back to the horizon when she stood. Hagar heard mutters as Seti explained, "It's only a sky picture. There is no water."

"It makes me feel cooler, somehow," Hagar told those nearby and saw that they understood her Canaanite.

When they again started forward words tumbled over each other as almost everyone discussed the mirage. Then the sound of harps, flutes, and singing rose from the caravan. The waves of sound rolled and echoed, built and diminished. It was a sand melody, a song to fit the immense, boundless, lonely land. Hagar saw that the music soothed the weary animals. Her tired donkey walked less stiffly in the pull and yield of the sand.

At last they rode into an area where boulders and loose shale covered the slopes. The colors of the cliffs struck Hagar with their sheer beauty. The caravan came to a halt. Squares of woven goat hair fastened to poles provided individual families with a small patch of shade. The rocks, now too hot to sit on, gave off an intense heat. Hagar began to look for Sarai.

"Share my shade and food," she said when she saw the girl. "Later we'll come to a well."

Hagar placed cheese and olives on her bread. "Wells and water are magic words."

"They are in the desert, but we have sufficient water if we meet no emergency."

"Sarai, you're so kind to all these people."

"El Shaddai wants us to be. We love to please Him."

"I thought of El Shaddai as I rode along."

"What made you think of Him?"

"I remembered my resolve to follow you and El Shaddai."

"I'm glad. Let's close our eyes and rest. The caravan will pause here for a while."

Later she searched for some sign of the well ahead. When the long shadows in the recesses of the cliffs had turned to violet the caravan stopped and began to remove the covering stones of the well.

Word passed along the line that the flocks had been watered and were still traveling. Those at the front of the caravan replenished their water supplies and rode on to give others access to the well. After Amon Re disappeared from the sky the caravan traveled in the evening coolness for a time then stopped. By the light of the moon, her muscles stiff, Hagar rolled out her sleeping mat on the sand. Before she slept she heard sun-heated rocks, cooling too quickly, explode like thunder. During the cold night she woke and tried to remember where she was. The odor of animals together with their noisy sleeping made her remember. For a time she listened to the night then dozed again.

Day after day followed each other in a nightmare of heat and dust, with each day hotter than the previous one. One day Abram rode back along the caravan and Hagar saw his concern as he scanned the horizon and sniffed the wind. Messengers gave commands that left everyone's face tense and pale. The warning of a giant sandstorm, the Khamsin, flew from mouth to mouth.

The heat continued to grow worse and dominated the conversation. Everyone watched the southeast horizon. An ominous silence hung over the wilderness. The donkeys and camels became difficult to manage.

When a dark haze appeared on the horizon Seti ordered the caravan to form a large circle. As Hagar looked at the immense land studded by sand dunes dread began to edge into her heart. She felt helpless. Experienced caravaneers organized the animals within the circle and prepared to stay with them. Others unloaded the baggage and formed it into partially buried barriers. The fate of the caravan depended on everyone's strict obedience to orders. Every action had a purpose. Parents settled crying infants, children, and themselves together with food, water, rugs, mats, and blankets into low depressions behind the baggage barricades. The guide assigned guard duty to some fathers, while others he asked to care for the animals.

Hagar found Sarai telling the mother of a large family that she would stay with them in case they needed help. The woman and older children scooped a deep depression in the sand, spread rugs in the depression, and stacked baggage along the edge, the heaviest on the southeast side. Sarai motioned for her to help them. Then to the mother, she said, "Where are your tent curtains packed?"

She pointed, and Sarai and Hagar untied the ropes and pulled out the longest goat hair curtains and stretched them over the baggage. Then they tied them to the ropes around the stacked baggage. The children frantically pushed sand up around the baggage. Next, the mother tied squares of cloth around the nose and mouth of each child and sent them with bread and water underneath the tent curtains, instructing the older children to care for the younger. A glance to the southeast warned Hagar that time was running out. Sarai helped the mother tie her well-wrapped infant to the front of her with a large square of cloth. Hagar followed the example of those around her and tied a cloth square across her own nose and mouth. A gust of wind nearly swept them off their feet as Hagar asked if she could remain with Sarai.

The woman nodded, then added, "Stay on this side of me. The storm is almost on us."

In the southeast a boiling black cloud rose from the desert floor. Quickly it hid the face of Amon Re as instinctively the frightened animals lay down. The travelers, covered by anything available, stretched on the ground behind the baggage barricades.

Soon the shrieking storm swept through the desert. Hagar struggled to protect her head as she peeked at the storm. The sand-filled air walled her in. Those lying nearby resembled little more than slight mounds of sand.

The hot winds went wild with fury and howled like demons, pelting everyone with sand and stones. As sand piled on her, Hagar tried to shake it off and called to Sarai but the wind snatched away her words. Hour after hour the storm raged. She couldn't eat but occasionally managed to sip some water. Every so often she would push herself up on her knees to dump enough of the sand off to keep from being buried.

Finally it was night for she felt cold. When a guard shook her she peeked out at a shrouded figure who bent close and asked, "You all right?"

Hagar found enough voice to shout over the wind. "Yes." Rising, he leaned into the wind, swayed, and vanished, swallowed by a curtain of sand.

As night wore on she fought drowsiness and her eyes closed. For a few moments she roused and pushed off more heavy sand, slept, then unburied herself again. Again she felt sand heavy on her and wondered if she were turning to dust, if her Ba was escaping. Her eyes stung. Exhausted, she wanted to scream and tried. But no sound came from her scratchy throat. Was she in her eternal grave? No, Abram had said El Shaddai would help them survive the storm, because He had promised him a son not yet born. A thousand times she told herself, "Because of the promised son, it will be all right."

Three days the storm raged until the wind at last exhausted its fury. People and animals stood to their feet amidst dead birds sprawled on the sand. The contours of sand dunes had changed. Sarai, her clothing full of sand, went from mother to mother, offering help. The tears of children turned the sand on their faces to mud. Relieved that the storm was finally over, the travelers laughed at the dust in their beards, eyebrows, and hair. They brushed and slapped at each other's coatings of sand.

To appease their hunger they crunched dried bread flavored even more than usual with sand. Hagar washed hers down with water. Rejoicing broke out when word circulated that not one child had been lost. Every person and nearly all the animals were safe. She shared their exhilaration. Their baggage was safe though buried in miniature sand dunes. Dust still hid Amon Re, and sand-filled eyes, ears, and nostrils made her life uncomfortable.

After Abram offered a sacrifice of gratitude to El Shaddai for his protection, the caravan once more headed across the sand-rippled desert. As she listened to the plop, plop of tired animal feet Hagar dozed and dreamed of invisible spirits slinking around the sand dunes. Suddenly grief-stricken wails from the front of the caravan jolted her back to reality. A mournful lament flew along the line of travelers until the sadness echoed through the desert. With it came the order to halt. The bones of a small caravan lay uncovered by the storm. Its travelers had lost their lives in a previous storm. Astonished, Hagar wondered if their names had perished. *Are they lost forever? Can the desert really have such power?*

Seti gave orders to go around the tragedy. As Hagar rode past she saw Eliezer and servants collecting the uncovered flint knives, bows, and arrows to add to their own supply. They picked up camel leg bones and the larger bones of donkeys, cattle, and sheep to make needles, arrows, and handles for tools. From her donkey driver she learned that some of the servants would remain behind long enough to again bury the human remains in the sand.

Seti sent word that such bones are a desert sign post indicating that they were still on the right trail. If a caravan did not find any such remains, it was a signal that they might be lost. Seti told the travelers that Abram had gone ahead with several dozen fast camels to En-mishpat for water. He would return with enough to care for any emergency.

For several days fine dust continued to blow and partially obscured Amon Re and ground away at their spirits. When Hagar found the water skin empty she knew she had never before been so thirsty. She sympathized with children pleading for a drink. On all sides she heard concerns for the animals. Donkeys could go four days without water, camels 10. But both had suffered in the storm. Seti begged for patience. "We're not far from En-mishpat," he assured everyone.

Hagar's thirst made her lips crack and flake and her face felt like a clay mask. Because she didn't hear a word of complaint from Sarai she choked down her own. Late in the day Abram returned. Cheers sped along the caravan as its members learned that the flocks and herds were already grazing on hills above En-mishpat. They had survived with only minimal loss.

"We're less than a full day's journey from the wells of En-mishpat," Seti announced. Singing spread through the caravan and soothed the thirst-crazed animals.

En-mishpat

As they neared the oasis at En-mishpat the camels and donkeys increased their pace because of the presence of water. Hagar jolted each time her donkey jumped some obstruction. The air became easier to breathe as the dust settled. The terrain changed and hills resumed their clear-cut outlines. In spite of her weariness Hagar's anticipation grew.

Scattered across the hills Hagar saw Abram's numerous cattle, camels, donkeys, and sheep already grazing. The green-crowned palms against the brown hills made her feel less homesick. As they approached En-mishpat people came to gaze at the large caravan. Then all at once the villagers shouted a welcome.

Far ahead she saw the lead camel halt and kneel. "We'll water the animals and fill the water skins, then camp on the hill across from the village," her donkey boy explained.

Disappointed at being away from the village, Hagar asked why.

"We'll be above the mosquitoes."

"Good." She slapped at the insects that had begun to circle around her head. "Why are the houses in the village round?"

The boy smiled. "The shape protects against storms. Wind blows around them easier."

She watched Sarai's servants water the animals. When Sarai's camel crouched with legs folded, she mounted it. As the animal rose in four great lurches, Sarai leaned back then forward, now back and forward again. As Hagar laughed the woman joined in the merriment and said, "I'll see you on the hill." The girl followed and servants pitched her tent next to Sarai's.

"How long do we stay here?" she asked.

"At least 15 days. Both animals and people need rest."

Sitting on a rock, Hagar shook her hair. "Do you think we'll ever be able to wash all this sand out of our hair and clothes?"

"Most of it. Hagar, you seem tired."

"So tired I couldn't ride another day. Right now I'm so weary I wish I were a rock."

Sarai laughed. "A rock?"

Hagar patted the boulder she sat on. "I wouldn't need to eat, wash, or even sleep. I'd just rest and sit still a thousand years."

Abram's wife chuckled as she shook sand from a rug. "Tomorrow you'll be ready for anything. Look who's coming."

The girl turned to see Khuni riding a black donkey. Weariness forgotten, she jumped to her feet to meet him.

"Khuni, I haven't seen you for days. Did you get caught in the sandstorm?"

"Yes, but we arrived here three days ago." He slid from the donkey.

Hagar noted the lines in his face and that his body slumped from fatigue. "Was it rough?"

"Day and night we fought to keep the sheep from being buried alive. Sheep are stupid, they just lie down to die, but camels are smart. They kneel and wait out the storm." He remounted, and as he rode off, he said, "I'll look for Meret and her family. I've a message for her father."

"Tell Meret I'll visit her when I'm not helping Sarai," the girl called after him.

Hagar unrolled her mat near the entrance of the tent and watched as the setting sun turned the dust-laden air the color of blood and fire as if a sacrifice were being offered to El Shaddai. The sand below caught the tint of the flaming sky. Long shadows crept across the desert.

After a few whispered words to El Shaddai, she poured water from the water skin on her hands, ate some pressed figs, then lay on her mat with her face toward the direction of Egypt. The storm had shredded her head covering so she took another from a nearby basket. The bark of jackals grew fainter and she closed her eyes.

Awakened by voices, Hagar pushed herself up on her elbow to see some servants building a stone altar in the light of dawn. She knew that some of the friendly villagers would later share Abram's worship. Staring at the houses in the distance, she decided she would visit the settlement today. After she washed her face, neck, and arms, Sarai's maid, Inara, came to braid her hair.

"We have much work to do," Sarai said when she saw Hagar. "Come with me."

The girl followed her to a rocky area. "See these cuplike depressions worn into the limestone rock? The women of En-mishpat grind barley in them by pounding the grain with a rolling motion. You may mill flour in one of them. The barley has just been harvested. Today the bread will be especially good. We'll make new cheese also. While we wait here for the sheep and cattle to grow fat again we'll eat well."

Hagar worked with Inara, a servant from north of Damascus who knew Amorite, the language of Canaan. As they ground the grain together she taught Hagar new words and sentences. Hagar liked the odor of the crushed barley. Hard as milling flour was, it still was more enjoyable than riding donkeys and camels.

"Inara, I'd like to see the houses in En-mishpat. Do you think Sarai will go to the village?"

"Yes, she plans to visit the women."

"When?"

"I think soon. I'm sure she will take us along if our work is done."

Later Sarai announced, "Hagar, you and Inara milled enough flour that you have time to join me when I go to the village with some of the other women."

The walk to the village was pleasant since it had turned cooler after the storm. As they approached the settlement women and a flock of children rushed out to meet them. Some of the women already knew Sarai. Hagar recognized the similarity of their language to Amorite. The villagers communicated as much with their faces and hands as with their lips. Since Hagar understood little of the conversation she studied the circular stone houses. To her they resembled pyramids whose tops were round instead of pointed. Each house had a walled courtyard and narrow alleyways between them.

A villager invited Sarai and her attendants into one courtyard. Inside close to the wall grew a few herbs. Their hostess arranged for a young girl to serve them boiled milk in thick pottery cups. The flat barley cakes were good even though they contained a little extra sand. The women asked Sarai many questions and Hagar heard her speak of El Shaddai. She wished she understood what Abram's wife was telling them.

As the days went by both the animals and the people lost their gaunt looks. Hagar saw Abram at the morning sacrifice and again at the evening meal. During the day he inspected his flocks and herds. Whenever she had a chance Hagar visited with Meret, while Khuni was on a far hill with the sheep.

One evening Abram announced, "Nearby is a hill with good flint. A group of 50 men will go there tomorrow to make arrows and tools. They'll stay three days so Sarai will send some women to cook for them."

Sarai chose two older women then turned to Hagar. "You and Inara may go. When you are not cooking, do whatever Eliezer tells you."

At dawn they left on fast camels for the mountain, where gleaming flint chips dotted the hillside. Hagar was elated to find Khuni in the group. The men selected a spot to work, then settled themselves to eat. As Hagar distributed food she especially noticed one small group of men. One individual seemed different than the others. At first she thought it was the way he sat erect on a boulder. He was taller than the four shepherds with him. But there was something else. His desert-browned face was set apart from the rest by his carefully trimmed beard. The tone of his voice, his appearance, his self-assured behavior—all conveyed the impression that he was someone to be reckoned with.

When all the men had left for their work Hagar asked one of the women about him and learned that he was Lot, Abram's nephew. Hagar was glad that Khuni had come along since he could explain things in their Egyptian language. During a midmorning rest period she inquired why the men were digging chunks of stone out of the ground instead of just picking up chunks of flint.

"The stone in the ground is easier to work. The flint on top of the ground Amon Re has already hardened."

"Do you know how to make flint tools?"

"Abram permitted me to come so I can learn. Eliezer will show me how."

Later Hagar watched as Eliezer demonstrated to Khuni how to wrap a piece of leather around his left hand to protect his fingers. With his right hand he picked up a chunk of flint and gripped it with the leather. "The chipping starts from the edge," Eliezer explained. He pressed against the flint with a tool made from a deer's antler. Then a downward and forward push forced flakes of flint to fly off. By working round and round with the horn tool he shaped the flint into a point.

Eliezer pointed to the horn in Khuni's hand. "You can control the size of the chip you break off by the way you use this tool."

Hagar watched the younger man pry off chip after chip. "This is fun," he said.

"Good," Eliezer continued. "Sometime, try obsidian. It chips easier and makes the sharpest points known."

Khuni flaked from the point to the base to produce an arrowhead. "Hagar, look." He held it up for her inspection.

"What will you make next?"

"I'll try a spearhead. I believe I can chip faster now."

Eliezer reached for the arrowhead. He turned it around, rubbing his thumb over its smooth surface. "Fine, Khuni. Fine. Now place it in the hot sun to season."

For three days Hagar watched the men fashion scrapers, pear-shaped mace heads, axe heads, fine blades, spears, knives, and arrowheads, some with barbed or serrated edges. Eliezer, a gifted stone-worker, produced fine flint sickle blades. These he would later embed in camel-bone handles. Then he chipped a flint knife for each of the women. Hagar felt the keen edge on hers. She wanted to show Sarai the beautiful white streaks in the brown stone blade.

At Eliezer's request the women packed the finished tools between layers of wool and laid them in baskets. When the toolmakers returned they met Abram, Sarai, and others coming from a farewell given in their honor in En-mishpat.

As Hagar halted her donkey near Sarai Abram drew Eliezer and his camel to one side. "For three days I've inspected the animals," she heard him say. "The herds are ready to go. Let's send them on to Bethel tomorrow. The next day the caravan will follow."

"I'll send messages to the chief shepherds and herders," Eliezer replied.

"Have them meet at my tent this evening. Ask Lot to come also."

Khuni edged his donkey toward the two men. "Eliezer, I can take your message to the eastern hills. I'm going there now."

Abram's chief servant smiled at the boy. "They're quite far away. Take a fast camel."

With a wave of his hand Khuni rode off to get a fresh camel grazing on a nearby hill.

Eliezer turned back to Abram. "That boy already speaks the Amorite tongue like a native."

The patriarch gazed after Khuni. "I was impressed when he and his grandfather, Baufra, visited me in Egypt."

Back at Sarai's tent Hagar showed her the knife blade. She turned it over and felt the sharp edge. "This is beautiful. Eliezer makes fine knives." Handing it back to Hagar, she said, "When it has a handle let me try it."

"Eliezer will make a handle from some bones he found in the desert," Hagar said. She studied Sarai. The time they had spent at En-mishpat had erased the woman's weary look. Sarai returned Hagar's gaze, and as if reading her heart, said, "This rest has been good for you. You no longer seem homesick for Egypt."

Hagar thought a moment. "I don't think I am." She held out her hands. "Look, no more blisters. Each day I feel stronger."

Sarai nodded. "The day after tomorrow we leave. There'll be desert but we'll travel north by the 'Way of the Wells.'"

"Way of the Wells?"

"The wells are a short day's journey apart. We'll stay overnight at each of them."

Hagar went to her tent to pack and then watch Amon Re disappear in the west. Shadows hid the contours of the land and a gentle breeze blew. When she finished packing she sat in the tent entrance. She still felt jubilant at having survived the sandstorm. *I'm now a Sand-dweller,* she told herself. *I've swallowed wind and sand.*

"Hagar."

Startled, she wheeled around to see who had spoken. "Khuni! I didn't see you approach."

He sat down on a rock. "I took a short cut. hoping I'd find you here. Do you like a Sand-dweller's life?"

"So far. I've been thinking that I should stop speaking of Amon Re and call the sun by its Canaanite name."

"I'm glad I joined Abram's caravan. To follow his El Shaddai was the best decision I ever made."

"Why?"

"You see how great Abram is—honest, courageous, and kind. He says anything good about him comes from El Shaddai. I want to be like Abram and his God." Neither of them said anything for several moments.

Hagar studied Khuni. "Have you decided to be a shepherd?"

His eyes were frank. "No, I'll be a trader like Abram. If I have sheep my servants will care for them."

"Will you take a caravan back to Egypt?"

His eyes shot instant fire. "I want my family to know about El Shaddai."

"Does He mean that much to you?"

"Everything."

Hagar saw no loneliness, only joy in her childhood friend as he used a stick to draw a crude picture in the dust at his feet. "I never knew I'd enjoy hard work so much," he said.

"Khuni, weren't you afraid during the sandstorm?"

"Not much. There wasn't time. I constantly brushed sand off my band of sheep. Abram had wisely sheared them. Then he gave them time to grow just enough new wool to protect their skin from the sun. Sand in their wool would have made a load so heavy that they'd have lain down and waited for death."

"Did you lose any?"

"Only one old ewe. Were you afraid?"

"I was afraid, but I was close to Sarai."

"You still like her?"

"Just as you do Abram."

"I wish all Egyptians were like they are. You've heard that El Shaddai promised them a son?"

"Yes, a son whose descendants will be kings. Won't that be wonderful?"

"I hope the son is like his father."

Hagar sighed. "I'm sure he will be."

To Luz

At dawn the villagers lined the trail shouting farewell. Hagar, fighting her sudden sadness, fussed to herself about the sand and dust kicked up by the animals. "Sand, always sand in my eyes, ears, and mouth," she grumbled. Then new tears burst forth and she rubbed her grimy hands against her eyes. *A wise pharaoh said "a heart is trained by knowledge,"* she thought, *but Sand-dwellers train mine.* The warm sun made her feel peaceful. *Sarai always seems happy, and she says it comes from attitudes that she's learned from El Shaddai. I want to be gentle and good like Sarai.* She watched the rising sun drink the night's mist and dew, warm the breeze, and bronze the western hills. Ahead lay a burned out, wind-sculptured landscape.

After a half-day's journey they met a caravan winding south to En-mishpat. The camel drivers stopped to exchange greetings and discuss travel conditions. Hagar found their foreign tongue impossible to understand. She laughed in delight at the black-eyed children, swathed in blankets and lashed to the camels. Small lambs thrust their heads from some of the donkey loads. Women and older children fanned out on either side of the road, searching for dried dung to fuel their evening fire. The caravan was on its way to Egypt, and for a moment homesickness threatened to overwhelm her.

Abram's caravan continued northeast, following the meandering trail. Mirages danced on the horizon. On her right the hills swept endlessly to the horizon. That night by the wells of Bir Hofir she slept under the stars while the sand radiated the day's heat. Not even the wind could keep her awake.

A donkey braying close to her head woke her. Stiff and sore, she rolled up her bed and limped with it to the donkey. Remembering the caravan that they had encountered the day before, she wondered if Khuni would lead a similar one along the "Way of the Wells" to the land of the Nile.

As her caravan prepared to leave, Hagar quickly swallowed some bread and a bowl of fermented sheep's milk. At first she walked on crusted sand that crumbled beneath her feet and watched an eagle circle over the hills. The procession wound around giant rocks heavily eroded by wind-driven sand. When the heat of the sand grew too intense, Hagar mounted her donkey. The caravan plunged into one mirage after another.

Then Hagar noticed a strange silence that began to make everyone uneasy. "A storm is coming," her donkey driver warned. When a bank of yellowish gray loomed on the horizon shouts of "Lie down" raced through the caravan. Everyone forced the nervous animals to the ground, then threw themselves down beside the creatures for protection. Soon the air vibrated to a continuous roar that grew constantly louder. A great black and menacing cloud wheeled overhead, blotting out the sun and dumping sand and a host of buzzing insects on the caravan. The wind-devil struck—then vanished. Bleeding men and women, cut by debris hurled by the winds, now struggled to their feet. Seti assessed the damage.

Hagar joined Sarai and others in aiding the injured. They passed out wet cloths to protect sandblasted faces from the sun. The wind-driven sand had shaved the hair from one side of some of the camels and donkeys. The men began to adjust their packs so as not to injure the animals any further.

The next five days passed routinely as the caravan traveled from well to well. The villages of Resisim, Ain Nureifig, Isbeita Rehobat, and Elusa all resembled each other. But enjoying their hospitality broke the monotony of the journey. Their encounters with other merchant caravans offered moments of excitement, especially if Abram traded with them.

Hagar enjoyed the constant change of the desert. Sometimes the swirling sand quickly obliterated their tracks. At other times they rode through scrubby trees in rocky wadis. Then again the caravan might wind around hills and overlook other wadis. They eased through a plain littered with black rocks with never a glimpse of vegetation. Instead, yellow and black scorpions lived there. Multicolored limestone and sandstone cliffs sometimes bordered the rocky landscape. The trail twisted past eroded outcroppings of rock. Finally Hagar spotted the Beersheba Basin where they would rest for three days. Abram's flocks and herds had already arrived and grazed in its fields.

The hard journey over, they set up camp near a wadi that still had a few wet season springs. Hagar hadn't seen so much water since leaving Egypt. She knelt and dipped her hands in the water, lifting handfuls to splash on her face. Here they could bathe, wash hair, and launder clothes.

Back at camp, Sarai told her, "The desert part of the journey is over. The way to Luz will be easier except for a stretch of mountains."

Hagar picked up three small green balls and began to juggle them. Sarai smiled at her. "Don't try to eat those *'gefen sadeh.* They're poison."

Hagar flung the gourds away. "When they turn orange and hard, however, they can be used as medicine," Sarai added.

The girl stretched her arms above her head. "Is Luz as nice as this?"

Sarai's eyes sparkled. "Yes, we'll live near where we did before going to Egypt. I'll be so glad to be home." She threw out her arms to take in all the land. "Someday all this will belong to Abram's descendants."

Hagar looked closely at her. "How do you know?"

The woman sat down on a mat. "El Shaddadi promised it to him."

"Khuni says El Shaddai promised you and Abram a son. Aren't you too old?"

Sarai's face grew grave. "I hope the promised one comes soon for I am growing older." Her eyes seemed to gaze inward as she whispered to herself, "I'll be a mother of kings."

"I'll be your son's nurse. I love children."

With a laugh Sarai jerked back to reality around her. "We'll see when he's here."

"The wife who bears a king in Egypt is favored and can have

anything," Hagar said seriously. "Your God must love you."

Sarai's mouth tightened. "I just want a son."

Noticing the approach of Abram, Hagar announced, "I'm going to Inara's tent."

Inara was constantly busy. Her expressive eyes could fill with sorrow or overflow with joy. At times they chastised or commanded.

"Hagar, I'm glad you came. I need help spinning this wool."

Although Hagar picked up a spindle and began twisting the wool, she soon became frustrated at her clumsiness. "There are so many things I can't do."

Inara untangled it and handed it back. "You learn fast. Sarai is pleased with your progress."

"Sarai is looking for a son that El Shaddai promised to Abram."

"I know. They've been waiting for years."

"Aren't they too old."

"It seems so, but El Shaddai has made the promise more than once."

After a few minutes Hagar began to get the knack of the spindle. "Why doesn't He keep His promise?"

"I don't know but I think He will. Have you noticed how Abram likes children? He plays with them. Children always run to meet him. He should be a father."

Their three days in the Beersheba Basin soon ended. The last wisps of smoke from the cooking fires drifted in the evening breeze, and frogs provided background music for the evening sacrifice. Moths spread their wings and flew into the night. Hagar loved the evening fire when Abram's clan gathered together. It had a feeling of peace and security.

The flocks and herds were already on their way when they broke camp the next day. The caravan turned northeast through hill country where the trees delighted Hagar. She watched the sun glint on pine needles and enjoyed the shade of oaks. Egypt had few trees, and a forest was a new experience to her. She exclaimed over the fragrant henna blossoms, scarlet anemones, and white lilies. The acacia strap-flower trees appeared to be on fire with flame-colored blossoms. She learned the names of trees and plants from her donkey driver. Bird songs filled the air and flocks of migrating birds flew north. Before long the caravan rode through a narrow gorge onto the plain of Mamre.

After a day and a half they arrived at a plateau between Luz and Ai. Hagar's eyes drank in the greenness stretching to the broken hills in the east. The gentle wind rippled the grass. Bees hummed around the blossoming "Wake-trees" (almond trees). "Is this where Sand-dwellers live?" she exclaimed. "It's beautiful."

The caravan once again set up its tents in a great circle. Hagar helped Sarai while the servants leveled the ground, then placed reed mats on the floor and finally thick rugs. Heavy curtains divided the tent into two compartments. The servants hung rich tapestries portraying scenes from Ur of the Chaldees upon the walls. In one room Sarai placed her sleeping mat, clothes chests, and music instruments. In the other compartment servants placed low tables and chests containing food utensils. A pile of sitting mats rested beside the entrance. More servants constructed a fire pit nearby.

Hagar surveyed the tent. "I think it's elegant."

Sarai laughed. "You're used to temples and palaces. Are you sure you'll feel at home?"

"My home will ever be where Abram and Sarai spread their carpets."

Sarai pointed to a water jar beside the entrance. "There's water to wash people's feet before they enter. To help keep the tent clean no one may walk inside with sandals or dust on their feet." Then she knelt beside a chest to remove pottery. "I sent servants to help you fix your tent."

"Come see mine when it's finished," Hagar said as she left.

"You'll be comfortable here," Sarai said later when she came to inspect the tent. Then she picked up a small statue. "This is Sen Wosret?"

"Yes, so I can remember him." Seeing the look in Sarai's eyes, Hagar hastened to add, "I don't worship him."

The woman replaced the statue. "Tomorrow Dendera and Inara will begin to teach you many things. You'll be busy."

When Sarai left Hagar went to rest in the shadow of a rock behind her tent. Doves cooed in distant trees. She watched the still-loaded camels and donkeys near the entrance to the camp. Children squealed while they played or helped their parents. The noise flushed quail from the nearby bushes and the birds ran to hide in the grass. It brought back memories of quail in Egypt, which made her hungry. She pictured the pyramids, the temples, and the palaces of her homeland. Her memories of Egypt had grown dim in the desert. Then her thoughts led her to the altar near Abram's tent. Finding a stick, she began to draw hieroglyphs in the dirt. *Why should El Shaddai, who is greater than any god, have only a pile of rocks for a temple?*

"Hagar, don't you ever work?"

She looked up to see Khuni. "My work begins tomorrow. Why aren't you with the shepherds?"

"I was—helping them build fences of brush to corral the sheep and cattle at night."

"They're done already?"

"Oh, they're not finished. The shepherds are still working on them. But they had enough people there and didn't need me at the moment."

"Lucky you. Will you always work with the shepherds?"

He shrugged. "Tomorrow I'll help the men set up an eight-pole tent to store the supplies and merchandise unloaded from the camels and donkeys."

"Khuni, do you miss Egypt?"

The boy thought a moment. "I miss my family. I wish they were here, but I like these people."

Hagar glanced up from her drawing. "You sound happy."

"I suppose so. I learn so much here." He studied her face. "You look content."

Just then Eliezer blew the shophar summoning the camp to worship. In a few moments the entire camp assembled and Abram sacrificed the lamb. The ritual mingled both sadness and joy in her, a reaction she couldn't quite explain.

Abram called for El Shaddai's help as he once again camped in this spot. After his prayer, he announced, "Since we will remain her for the time being, I'll use the opportunity to tell you more about El Shaddai. We know that the living God created us and the world around us. A God of infinite wisdom, He gave humanity the right to make its own choices. El Shaddai offers us wisdom to make the right choice in any matter if we will but pray for His guidance."

As she listened to Abram her heart longed for wisdom. She looked at the stars dusting the heavens above. The crescent moon would soon vanish behind the western hills. The vastness of El Shaddai's sky made her feel small, insignificant. Eternity seemed to stare her in the face—she felt that she could almost touch it.

"El Shaddai promises that Sarai and I will have a son, and his descendants will inherit this land," Abram continued. "God has told me that He will bless the whole world through my offspring." Abram paused to let his hearers catch the importance of his words. A murmur of approval rose from his listeners. "May you sleep well, for tomorrow we work," he concluded.

Abram and Lot Separate

◫◫◫◫◫◫◫◫◫◫◫◫◫◫◫◫◫◫◫◫◫◫◫◫◫◫◫◫

Hagar walked up a slight rise behind her tent. From there she could watch the camp awaken to a new day. Scarlet anemones splashed color across the land. On impulse she hurried to the tent for her harp and sat with her back to a small tree near the entrance. As she plucked the strings she closed her eyes and pictured herself beside the lotus pool in the palace of the women. She remembered the songs that Baufra loved and the ones she had performed before Pharaoh. The notes on the harp leaped from her fingers. Then she heard her own voice, strong and clear, sing one song after another. She became lost in a world of music and pure joy. But finally sensing the presence of others, she opened her eyes to amazed faces clustered in a semicircle around her. Blinking in embarrassment, she stood and clutched her harp against herself.

Sarai smiled at her and Abram said, "A voice worthy to perform for a king. You must learn the songs of your new home." A small girl shyly touched the harp. Hagar felt that she was now truly part of this new world of the Sand-dwellers.

The shofar sounded for the morning sacrifice, dispersing the group. After the ritual Sarai said, "Hagar, remember that today we're going to the market in Luz. We'll leave as soon as we've eaten."

Luz was a bewildering blur of sights, sounds, and smells—particularly smells. Merchants hawked dried fish, dried fruits, vegetables, pottery, fabrics, furniture, oil, and grain. The group from Abram's camp separated to shop in the various parts of the market.

Hagar followed Sarai and her servants through the narrow streets, picking their way around piles of manure. Many shopkeepers cried out greetings to Abram's wife, beckoning her to check their wares. At one of the pottery stalls Sarai selected a supply of cups, bowls, cooking pots, water jars, and water basins to replace those broken during their journey to Egypt. As the merchant provided each person with a cup of water he kept repeating, "You honor me by coming to my humble shop." Sarai told Batanai, one of her servants, to handle the bargaining.

The merchant pointed to the pile of pottery. "Abram's wife has chosen well. All this for only 10 shekels of silver."

Batanai scowled. "My mistress will pay five shekels."

In dismay the merchant cried, "No, not enough. Not enough. Excellent pottery." He tapped one of the jars with a stick. "See the best. Nine shekels."

Amused, Hagar saw a glance pass between Sarai and Batanai. "My mistress offers six," the servant said.

The merchant threw out his arms and with an expression that was half scowl exclaimed, "How's a man to live." He squinted at them. "But for friends I sell for eight."

Sarai moved as if to leave while Batanai sighed and shook his head. Motioning to Sarai to follow, he started to leave. The merchant grabbed Batanai's arm. "Just a moment. For Abram, a friend, seven. A steal, I tell you, a steal."

Sarai with a smile nodded her consent. Batanai paid the merchant the seven shekels, which he received with smiles and profuse thanks. Batanai and his helpers soon had the pottery packed in baskets on the donkey's backs. They bid the merchant farewell and headed out into the commotion of the street. When they had finished their particular shopping they met the other members of the caravan at the east gate of the city.

As they walked along Hagar asked Sarai, "Why do people argue about prices?"

Sarai glanced at her. "Don't they in Egypt?"

"Yes, but why?"

"Merchants think a person who pays the first price is stupid. The pottery merchant came down to make us feel good."

Hagar laughed. "Then you raised your offer to make him feel good?"

Sarai nodded, then pointed. "Look, olive groves. There'll be a good oil supply this year. And we call the almond trees wake-trees, because they bloom first and wake up the ground."

During the following days Hagar helped weave, tan leather, dye wool, and grind flour. Then she supervised milling and laundering. The list was endless, demanding constant attention. But the herds and flocks had priority. The pastures had not fully recovered from the drought. Abram had to negotiate with the local landowners for additional grazing rights.

The Caananites and Perizzites pastured their own herds among the hills, reducing the land available to resident aliens such as Abram and Lot. As summer progressed the days grew hotter. Because it was the dry season, the land would not receive any rain until fall. Tempers flared among the shepherds as the seasonal springs dried up. The grass withered. Hagar heard increasing rumors about discontent between the shepherds of Abram and Lot. Soon the men brought their disputes to the two men for them to settle.

One day Hagar and Sarai sat fanning themselves in front of Sarai's tent during the afternoon rest period. Abram joined them. "Sarai, this problem of pasture for our herds has reached a crisis." Then he glanced at Hagar.

"It's all right," his wife said. "Hagar knows the camp problems."

He rubbed his hands together. "Eliezer thinks that the quarrels of the shepherds tend to reflect Lot's attitude. He's determined always to obtain the best for his flocks and herds."

Sarai stopped fanning. "Is that true?"

"Yes. Lot has been like a son, but I'm aware of a selfish streak in him."

"What can you do?"

"If the shepherds would only remain calm until the rainy season begins. Then the pastures will revive."

Just then Abram and Sarai glanced in the direction of what sounded like an argument. Hagar saw Eliezer approaching with Abram's and Lot's chief shepherds. Sheepskins hung from the men's shoulders and their leather belts held slings made of goat hair. Fire flashed in their eyes and they thumped their staffs into the ground.

Hagar rose, positioned mats for the men, then followed Sarai into the tent where they listened to the conversation.

Eliezer's voice showed his concern. "Abram, as you know the men are constantly quarreling over pasture rights." He paused as curious members of Abram's householders gathered around. Hagar and Sarai moved to the entrance where they remained silent observers.

When all were quiet Abram said, "Before I hear them, Eliezer, tell how you see the problem."

The chief steward pounded his right fist into his left palm. "In spite of the fact that you support Lot, he claims first rights to the best pastures. Despite all that you've given him, now he wants more."

Abram winced and turned to one of the men. "Merrhis, as Lot's chief herder, what do you say about your shepherds?"

The man could not hide his embarrassment. His dark eyes smoldering, he snapped, "We scramble for pasture and water every day."

"That's normal in summer," Abram agreed.

"But when we find some decent pasture we have grazing rights to, your shepherds say we're not fair and try to take it from us." Ill at ease, he lapsed into silence as he stared at the ground.

"Bathiah, how are my shepherds and herdsmen faring?"

Reluctantly he answered, "When we have good pasture, Lot's shepherds try to push us out, claiming it's theirs. This happens often."

In a voice as hard as flint, Merrhis replied, "When we reserve it, rights belong to us."

Abram remained silent for a moment, studying the men, then said, "The time has come for drastic action. Tell Lot to see me right after sacrifice in the morning. Accompany him." A low buzz of excited voices rose from the observers.

By the time Lot and the chief shepherds arrived at Abram's tent the next morning, the day had already begun to heat up. Abram, Eliezer, Lot, and the others climbed to the top of a nearby hill.

Hagar threaded a bone needle and started to sew while Sarai worked on a cloak for Abram. The girl felt the tension in her and saw her eyes stray toward the hill to which the men had gone.

When the men returned, Bathiah and Merrhis hastened to their duties while Lot faced Abram. "I'll leave now for the Jordan valley to

make the arrangements, then my people will pack when I return."
He turned to Sarai. "Uncle Abram has been most kind. My people
will say farewell at the evening meal fire before we leave."

Abram picked up a jug of water, poured some in a cup and the
rest on the ground, then hurled the cup to the ground, smashing it to
bits. Hagar and Sarai both jumped at the loud crash. Abram and Lot
stood in silence, searching each other's face. Then Abram said, "That
cup is a symbol of our relationship. It is now broken. It may never
be renewed. You, the son of Haran my dead brother, have been a
son to me." Abram embraced Lot and the two men wept. "May you
and your people go with El Shaddai's blessing."

For a time Lot could not speak. "I'm grateful for your fatherly
care," he said finally. "I'll always remember it."

"May you renew your strength." Lot reached for the cup of water
that Abram offered. "I'll walk with you to your camp."

When Abram and Lot departed, Sarai turned to Eliezer. "Don't
go. Tell us what happened. Is he leaving?"

Eliezer glanced at Hagar. "Would it be best to speak to you
alone?" he asked Sarai.

"No, Hagar now belongs to the household."

Eliezer sat cross-legged on a mat and Sarai stopped sewing to listen to him. "Sarai, your husband is a most unselfish man." The stew-
ards's strong hands slapped his knees. Then he pressed his fingers
together until the knuckles turned white. "I hope . . ." He paused. "I
hope Abram didn't make a mistake this morning."

"What do you mean?" Sarai demanded.

"He has good judgment and an understanding heart." Again
he stopped.

"Tell us everything," she persisted.

"Bathiah, Merrhis, and I stood a short distance behind Abram
and Lot. There we could see much of the land El Shaddai has
promised to Abram."

"It is a beautiful land," Sarai said. "So bountiful."

"With Lot beside him, Abram proposed his plan. He said, 'Let
there be no strife I pray you, between me and you, and between my
herdsmen and your herdsmen for we are brothers. Isn't the whole

land before you? Separate yourself from me. If you take the left hand, then I'll go to the right. If you depart to the right, then I'll go to the left.'"

Hagar almost gasped aloud, for Sen Wosret in Egypt would never give anyone under him a choice. She wondered why Abram had when he was Lot's superior. Then she heard Sarai ask, "Which did he choose?"

"Neither the left nor the right."

"Did Lot let Abram choose first?"

"Lot should have yielded the choice to his benefactor, but he didn't. He looked neither to the right nor to the left. For a long time he stared down on the valley of the Jordan." Eliezer glanced at Hagar. "From a distance it reminds me of the well-watered delta where the Nile separates into many rivers." The steward hesitated, then announced, "Lot chose the plain of Jordan."

Sarai's voice held unbelief. "The plain of Jordan? But it's not even part of the land El Shaddai promised."

The man nodded. "You know Abram hadn't even considered such a possibility, because of the wickedness there." Eliezer paused. No one interrupted the silence. Then he continued, "Abram is honored by rulers as a mighty prince, a wise and able chief. They even come at times to worship El Shaddai with him. Why couldn't Lot honor him. By choosing land not part of the Promised Land he—he rejects Abram."

"I fear for Lot. Abram had great plans for him. I doubt the people of Sodom will worship El Shaddai with Lot."

The steward jumped to his feet. "I see Abram returning. I must go to him."

Sarai put her hands over her face and sat in silence. Hagar busied herself picking up the broken pottery. Shortly Abram came to Sarai, looking tired and discouraged. When his wife heard his footsteps, she looked up. "So Lot is leaving."

With bitter disappointment in his voice, Abram said, "He chose the plain of Jordan. I fear for his wife and daughters."

Three nights later Lot and his family bid a tearful farewell. The next day he and his retainers left for the Dead Sea Valley. Late in the day Abram said to Sarai, "I'm going up on the hill. From there I can see Lot's people wind down into the plain. I think I'll stay and commune with El Shaddai there."

Next morning the shofar called the camp to the morning sacrifice earlier than usual. Hagar combed her hair and placed a band around it, then hastened to join the others at the altar. Abram, looking weary but happy, stood before his people. "Last evening El Shaddai spoke to me again. He said, 'Lift up your eyes, and look from the place where you are northward and southward. All the land you see I'll give to you and to your seed forever. I'll make your seed as the dust of the earth so that if a man can number the dust of the earth, then your seed can also be numbered. Arise, walk through the land in the length of it and in the breadth of it, for I'll give it to you.'"

Murmurs of approval spread through the crowd. "I'll leave Eliezer in charge here," Abram continued. "Then with a few men I'll walk through the land searching for pasture. When I return we'll move to better grazing grounds before our animals grow thinner and melt before our eyes."

The people began to cheer, but Hagar was not happy. She loved this place and did not want to leave.

When Abram returned sometime later, the camp pulled up stakes and traveled south to better grazing lands near Mamre.

War of the Kings

▯▯▯▯▯▯▯▯▯▯▯▯▯▯▯▯▯▯▯▯▯▯▯▯▯▯▯▯▯▯▯▯▯

As Hagar reached for Abram's empty bowl she heard running feet behind her. Abram stuffed the last fig in his mouth and stood to meet a camp guard with a travel-worn man. "Master Abram, news from Sodom," the guard announced.

"Quick, my Lord," the stranger gasped. "Lot and his family are prisoners of Ched-or-laomer. I only, Lot's servant, managed to escape." Hagar studied his dusty garments, his disordered hair, his bloodshot eyes and weary, hungry face, and felt that he could be trusted.

Abram, his voice sharp as flint, demanded, "What's this?" He turned to Sarai. "Bring this man water and something to eat."

The man gulped down the water. Abram's face was grim. "Tell me everything."

The messenger wiped his mouth with his hand. "Bera, Sodom's king, heard that Ched-or-laomer of Elam, and his allies had attacked Zuzim to the north, then Emin to the east. Both places had stopped paying tribute, so the Elamites punished them with a raid. Because Bera had halted their tribute two years ago, he organized a mutual protection pact with Birsha of Gomorrah, Shinab of Admah, Shemeber of Zeboiim, and the king of Belah. They would come to each other's aid should Ched-or-laomer's army return near Sodom to reach the 'King's Highway.' Our spies reported that Ched-or-laomer has plundered as far south as En-mishpat."

Abram winced. "We'd already heard about En-mishpat from some traders."

Lot's servant nodded. "Sodom's king and his army went out to meet Ched-or-laomer near the slime pits in the vale of Siddim" he continued. "The battle turned into a rout. Kings Bera and Birsha hid and those of the army still alive fled to the mountains."

"Did Lot join the fighting?" Abram demanded.

"No, he stayed in Sodom to help protect it. Raiders attacked the city. They took many captive as well as their possessions."

"How did you escape?"

"I was outside the city when I saw them, so I hid. When Ched-or-laomer's army headed north I came here."

Hagar brought food and more water and Abram stood. "We must rescue them," he said with determination. Then turning to a servant stacking wood near the altar, he ordered, "Find Eliezer. Tell him to come immediately.

"When you've finished eating, get some sleep," he told Lot's servant. "Meanwhile, we'll prepare to follow Ched-or-laomer." Abram hastened to his tent and moments later Eliezer and he were planning their military expedition. When Lot's servant finished eating, he joined them. As Hagar washed the empty bowl, Sarai emerged from her tent. She blinked back the tears threatening to spill and burst into a wail of grief.

"It's serious for Lot's family, isn't it?" Hagar asked. "Will they be slaves?"

"Unless they're rescued, I'm afraid for them."

"Can Abram save them? Those kings must have a large army."

"Pray that El Shaddai will help Abram," Sarai said. "But for now, go help Inara."

"Lot and his family have become captives of Elam's king," Hagar announced to the women grinding flour.

Exclamations of surprise, disbelief, and concern greeted her news. As Hagar milled more flour she watched the activity in camp gather momentum. A little later Batanai came for her. "Sarai requests your help," she said. "Go to her."

Tears streaked Sarai's face. Wanting to comfort her, Hagar grabbed her hands, kissed them, then sobbed through her own tears, "May I help?"

"Abram and Eliezer have organized 318 men to rescue Lot."

"That's not much of an army."

"He sent messengers to the treaty allies of the local kings. They'll bring their own troops."

"I hope their forces are large enough," Hagar worried.

Sarai caught her breath. "Don't be afraid. We must encourage the women whose husbands and sons will go with Abram. They'll be safe. Remember, the promised son hasn't yet come to Abram. Let's put our trust in El Shaddai."

Sarai was silent a moment, then said, "Dendera is too elderly to bear a lot of responsibility. I'd like you to take over some of her duties." Dendera was to the women servants what Eliezer was to the men. Although in Egypt Hagar had been trained in administrating a household, she just said simply, "I'll try."

"See that every household prepares food to last 10 days for each man—dried fruit, nuts, and roasted garbanzos. Have them bake enough bread for several days."

As Hagar went from tent to tent she found everybody on edge and talking louder than usual. Each woman accepted her instructions without question. The camp became a whirlwind of activity. After conveying Sarai's instructions to the last tent she encountered a group of men listening to Abram and Eliezer give them instructions. She lingered nearby, straining to hear as Abram issued commands to the men who would pass them on to still others. He directed the gathering of darts, slings, spears, and battle axes. Then Hagar returned to Sarai who sent her to supervise the packing of supplies.

Later, after helping Sarai with the evening meal, she sat before her tent pondering all that had happened. She thought it strange that Sarai and Abram did not condemn Lot or declare that his fate served him right. Neither did anyone else in the camp. As darkness crept over the hills Hagar huddled by the fire. A gentle breeze sent the flames dancing. Abram stood before the fire, waiting for his people. While Orion rose low in the east to chase the fleeing Pleiades, Abram's gaze sought the heavens above. He seemed to search for something beyond the stars. Suddenly he struck his chest with clenched fists and a cry escaped his lips. "May I find my brother's son, Lot, who is my son also."

The camp had now assembled. For a time no one said anything.

In the firelight Hagar saw the men's faces rigid with anxiety. Abram began to speak in a clear voice. "At Luz I tore myself from Lot, now he has been torn from me." A murmur rose from the men.

When it died, Abram continued. "You did well today preparing for the rescue. Word has reached us that the Amorite brothers Mamre, Eschol, and Aner will arrive with their armies tomorrow. We will leave at dawn the next day. The enemy will be five days ahead of us but all the captives and herds will slow them. We should be able to overtake them." Finally, he explained what those who remained behind in the camp should do while the men were gone.

As the crowd dispersed Hagar saw Khuni threading his way toward her. Hagar felt a twinge as she said, "So you did join an army."

Khuni's smile was forced. "This is only temporary."

"But the danger is real."

"Don't say that," Khuni snapped at her. "I'll return."

"You don't know that for sure."

"I do. While I've been with the flocks in the hills I've come close to El Shaddai. When I pray to him under the stars a peace fills my heart. I just know that I'll be all right."

"Sarai thinks Abram will return safely."

"I'm sure that he will, since he is 'El-Khalil,' the friend of El Shaddai."

"I'll pray for you. You must tell me all about it when you get back."

When Abram's army started northward, Sarai and Hagar and others climbed to the summit of a hill. As the column passed beneath them they waved and watched until the men disappeared into the distance. Hagar felt both excitement and a sense of infinite tragedy. Was she bidding goodbye to men who might not return? Tears washed down their faces as the women drifted back to camp.

The days dragged by with no word from the army. An unspoken fear settled over the camp. Hagar brushed away thoughts of death a dozen times a day. Several older men, their faces weathered and wrinkled, volunteered to guard the camp. Young boys with slings stationed themselves throughout the settlement, and others stayed with the shepherds and herders. Sarai, more than anyone else, was in charge, and she often needed Hagar's help.

One evening a runner drenched in sweat staggered to Sarai's tent and sank to the ground. Hearing the disturbance, women fearfully congregated in front of her tent. Hagar felt her heart begin to pound.

"Mistress," the messenger gasped, "Abram . . . Abram . . . has found the enemy."

"Did he save Lot?" she demanded.

"Not yet. He plans to wait until dark before attacking. Then he'll send another runner when he does."

After several moments of stunned silence, the women burst into wailing and lamentation. Fear overwhelmed Hagar. Someone died in every war. What if it were Khuni, Abram, or Eliezer? Gradually the shrill wailing faded and Abram's camp waited in silence.

The next day another messenger dashed into camp. A crowd rushed after him and Sarai left her tent and met him near the altar. "What has happened?" she demanded, grabbing his arm.

"Lot and the rest of the captives are free," he gasped. "Abram is pursuing the raiders."

"Is everyone safe?" the women shouted.

"I can't tell you more now. I must go to Bera, king of Sodom, with the news."

After more days of waiting the announcement of Abram's imminent return brought the camp out in mass. When guards spotted the approaching column pandemonium broke loose. The camp scavenger dogs began to howl and yap, and people scrambled up the slope to let the men pass. Dust made it difficult to recognize anyone, yet the women instinctively found their husbands and sons. Clinging to their arms the women followed the militia to camp.

When the camp had quieted somewhat, Hagar searched through the crowd until she found Khuni. Lapsing into Egyptian, she told him, "I've never seen such excitement."

"Hagar, I still can't get over what happened."

"You promised to tell me about it."

"I will but Abram will also tell everyone tonight."

She motioned toward an outcropping of rock.

He sat down wearily and forced a smile. "After five days we caught up with Ched-or-laomer's forces. The five kings had decided to rest and celebrate their victory. Abram divided his forces to approach the enemy from different directions. We took our positions while Ched-or-laomer's men were drunk and asleep. Just before dawn Abram sounded the trumpet signal to attack. They awoke in a panic, rolled from their tents like moths from cocoons, and scrambled for their weapons. Some ran away. The rest, terrified, attacked those near them, killing their own men."

Khuni hesitated, covered his eyes with his hands, then continued in a subdued voice. "They climbed over each other, trampling the fallen bodies. I will never forget the dreadful shrieks."

When he lapsed into silence, Hagar finally asked, "What happened next?"

Khuni took a deep breath and exhaled slowly. "Bodies lay everywhere. Abram took part of the troops and went after those who had escaped. He caught them near Hobah. The rest of us released Lot, his family, and the captives that we found tied up in tents near their camp. Then we rounded up flocks and herds without number. It took three days to bury the dead."

In a choked voice she asked, "Will their names be forgotten? Will they be as though they never were?"

"Abram says that El Shaddai knows where each man lies."

"I hope He doesn't forget."

As Hagar wiped at her tear-smudged face, Khuni said, "You won't believe what I'm about to tell you now."

"What do you mean?"

"When Abram returned to Dan we slowly headed back south. Melchizedek, king of Salem, met us near his city. He and his people brought us bread and wine. Because he is a priest of El Shaddai, Abram gave him a tenth of all the spoils we had captured. And Abram could have kept everything else for himself but he returned it and the hostages to Sodom's king."

Hagar gasped. "Pharaoh would never have done such a thing."

The boy nodded. "Abram wouldn't accept even a small part of the spoil. He said Mamre, Eschol, and Aner could have a share but the spoils from Sodom went to king Bera."

"I don't understand Abram," she declared. "Isn't he to be the father of kings? Shouldn't he gather wealth for them?"

Khuni was thoughtful. "I don't understand him either but I like the way he deals with others. He said El Shaddai gives him his wealth. Hagar, it seems strange but good to worship just one God. Even though He's invisible I sometimes feel His strong presence with me."

The Fifth Promise

Hagar snuggled under her sheepskins and listened to the wind rustle the leaves of the terebinth tree. She watched a band of light between the edge of the tent and the ground grow brighter and diffuse the darkness inside. Soon the strains of the shepherds' flutes floated down from the hills to the camp. She treasured such early morning moments when she had a chance to be alone for a few minutes and think through some problem or question.

One involved the issue of how to relate to Abram. He was quite different from her father. She had once believed her Pharaoh a superior being, a god and a mighty warrior. Sen Wosret's decisions, followed either by a sharp look or curt command, demanded instant results. His subjects bent to his every desire as he employed fear to secure respect.

On the other hand Abram won her respect by giving respect and by listening to the opinions of his people. He persuaded rather than forced anyone. *I prefer Abram's way,* she thought to herself as she stretched.

She sat up and began to make up her own words to a familiar tune.
"I live with beauty before me, with beauty beside me,
  With beauty above me, with beauty below me,
  With beauty around me, with beauty in Sarai's words,
  To spread beauty in me."

Slipping on a pair of low boots, she walked to the rock outcropping that partially shielded her tent from the wind. Kneeling, she inspected her wildflower garden that grew at its base. Khuni had brought the plants from the nearby hills. Having surrounded his own tent with such wildflowers and plants, he had shared some of them with her.

118

Behind the rock she picked some mint leaves and chewed on them. As she watered some of the herbs she remembered Baufra's gardens.

After the morning sacrifice, when the sun had soaked up the mist, she went to eat with Sarai and plan the day's work. Immediately she noticed the woman's red-rimmed eyes. "What is troubling you?" she asked cautiously.

Sarai shifted her position. "The recent war still disturbs Abram," she replied after a long moment of hesitation.

Hagar stopped the cup of goat milk midway to her lips. "But he won the war."

The woman stared out over the camp. "Yes, but he is a man of peace. The destruction of Elam's forces horrified him. He grieves over the action he had to take."

"Then why does Abram have an army?"

Sarai paused. "It consists only of our own men, and then just for protection against robbers and wild beasts."

"I don't understand. He saved Lot's family. El Shaddai helped him—so why does he grieve?"

"Abram says El Shaddai loved Ched-or-laomer and his allies."

Hagar's astonishment filtered into her voice. "He loved those cruel raiders?"

"Yes"—Sarai paused for emphasis—"El Shaddai loves everyone in the world. He wants all to choose unselfishness so war will be unnecessary. For this reason my husband doesn't want to be a man of war. He desires to dwell in peace and not become an object of vengeance or a revenger."

The girl sat speechless, letting her heart stretch to comprehend a God who loved His enemies. "Sarai, are you serious? Egyptian gods don't love their enemies. They kill those against them and make their names as though they never were."

"El Shaddai loves all people but He wants them and us to eliminate trouble by right choices with love." Sarai stood. "Last night El Shaddai again promised Abram a son and this land. Today, my husband will commune with El Shaddai."

Suddenly Hagar pointed. "Abram's leading a cow, a goat, and a ram up that hill."

"I know. He is to make a covenant with El Shaddai. If he's not back in time Eliezer will sacrifice the lamb tonight."

Before she could press for more details, Eliezer appeared with a group of young shepherds. Older men carrying tools met them at the supply tent. There she saw Khuni dispensing more tools.

Hagar picked up a water pitcher and towel. "I see the men will work on the cisterns and storage pits today."

Sarai held her right hand over a basin and the girl poured water over it. After she dried her hand she did the same for Hagar. The water left over Sarai then emptied on the herbs near her tent. "Check with me today if anything unusual happens."

When she reached her tent Hagar rolled up and tied the sides so a breeze could blow through it.

Before she arrived at the flour mill site she could already hear the scuff of millstones mixed with talk and laughter. Her crew of young girls and servants already toiled at their task of pulverizing a 10-day supply of barley flour. She set some to cracking sun-dried kernels of young boiled wheat and barley. When their clay jars were full they carried them to the food pits near the supply tent, climbed down a tricky ladder, and emptied the flour or crushed grain into larger jars. Then they returned to mill more.

When the shadows shrank and it became too hot to work she called a halt. The crew needed rest during the noonday sun. Back at her own tent she soaked some of the crushed wheat. Next she took from the storage basket the flint knife Eliezer had made and tested its sharp edge. She sliced new onions and fresh greens into a pot of lentils she had left cooking in a fire pit. Then she took handfuls of the soaked wheat, squeezed out the water, and added the grain to the lentils. When Inara emerged from her tent nearby she called to her, "Come eat with me."

"It smells delicious," Inara said, settling herself on a mat out of the sun under the edge of the tent. Hagar handed her a flat round of bread and set the lentil dish close to her. Together they tore the bread into pieces and used it to scoop up the lentil-wheat dish until they'd eaten their fill.

After glancing toward the eastern hills, Hagar said, "I see Khuni approaching. I hope he stops here."

Inara stood. "I'll go to my tent so you may speak your own language."

Hagar laughed. "Khuni prefers Amorite." Then she watched him enter the supply tent and come out swinging a bronze ax.

When he passed her tent she called out, "Sit in the shade with me. Why another ax?"

He chopped it into the dirt beside him. "To speed up the work."

"When will Abram have enough cisterns?"

"We'll always need more. There's always more animals and new people."

"Isn't the work hard?"

Khuni shrugged. "Sure, it's tough."

"Shouldn't slaves be the ones to excavate the cisterns? Pharaoh gave Abram slaves, and he already owned some."

Khuni stretched, then spoke in a mixture of Egyptian and Amorite. "You know how Abram is. He says that El Shaddai decrees equal respect both for the poor and the exalted."

A silence settled over them. She groped among her limited knowledge of Amorite for the right words. Shyly she said to him, "You're more handsome than you were in Egypt."

They sat staring at each other, tense and nervous. His hand reached out to pick up a twig and snap it. "Hagar, to me you are the most beautiful woman in either Egypt or Canaan."

She felt her heart leap around in her chest like a flopping fish. To compose herself she nervously toyed with the corner of the mat. When she glanced up Khuni sat gazing at the distant hills. For the space of many heartbeats she studied the serenity of his face.

Finally to ease the tension she felt, she asked, "What is Abram doing over on that hill?"

Khuni bowed his head and said, "Seeking a covenant."

Confused, she stared at him. "What do you mean?"

"Eliezer told us Abram took a heifer, a she goat, and a ram with him. He also took a turtle dove and a pigeon."

"To sacrifice?"

"No, he split each animal in half and laid them against each other. The birds he left whole."

"Why did he do that?"

"It's the custom, the way the people of this land seal covenants with each other."

"Sarai said he wants to make a covenant with El Shaddai."

He nodded. "True. While we worked on the wells we saw him chasing vultures and other birds away from the slain animals."

Hagar stood. "It's a strange custom." She paused. "I see my women are ready to work again."

Some she set to kneading and shaking cream in skin bags suspended from wooden tripods. When butter appeared the women separated it from the whey, boiled it, and put it in goatskin bottles. In warm weather it was like oil but Hagar liked it best in winter when it resembled candied honey.

Meanwhile some of the women heated sour milk to make cheese. When it curdled they drained it through cloth squares. The pressing molds extracted more liquid. Later they would use it as chunks, slabs, or slices. Some they would even shape into cheese balls.

That evening as the shadows lengthened Hagar and the others with her sang to calm their goats as they milked. Afterward they carried the milk into the tents where the cool night would keep it sweet until morning.

At the morning sacrifice Abram glowed with happiness. "El Shaddai spoke to me. Tonight I'll tell you His words."

As Hagar walked to her tent alone she found her heart full of questions. *Why should El Shaddai talk to Abram? Is it because God favors him or because he is a shrewd man? Or is it because he is honest and friendly to kings and servants alike? Who is Abram? He's not a god like Pharaoh. Egyptians consider him just a Sand-dweller. His friends here in Canaan know him as a merchant-prince, a wise and able chief. Ched-or-laomer found him a conqueror. And his people see him as the friend of El Shaddai.*

Inara came up behind her. "I wonder what El Shaddai told him."

"The last time El Shaddai spoke we left Luz," Hagar worried. "Will we move again?"

"Maybe El Shaddai spoke about the promised son," the servant suggested.

"But they're so old. Can they really have a son?"

The other girl hesitated. "El Shaddai can make it happen but it's been years since He first promised a son."

Hagar, wishing Khuni could hear what Abram had to say, asked, "Will they let some of the shepherds attend tonight?"

"They'll hear," Inara promised.

That night the flames of the campfire blew about in a fitful breeze, but Abram stood still and unwavering before his expectant people. As everyone grew silent, he said, "You know that since we rescued Lot I have feared that the people of this land might view me as a warlord. They would begin to distrust us and might even attack us lest we get too powerful. But the night before last El Shaddai told me in vision, 'Fear not I am your shield.'"

Hagar heard murmurs of approval. "Then I said, 'Lord, I'm childless,'" Abram continued. "'All the years of my married life I've longed for a son. Since I have no seed I can follow the custom of the land and adopt Eliezer. My servant will be my heir and become the father of the one to bless the world. He can receive my property, then care for Sarai and me in our old age.'"

Abram paused while he waited for the murmurs of surprise to cease. Hagar glanced at Eliezer across the fire. He sat cross-legged on his mat, apparently unmoved by the honor. "But," Abram resumed, "El Shaddai said, 'Eliezer shall not be your heir, only your own son. Go outside your tent.'

"Then he said, 'Look toward heaven. So shall your seed be. They shall inherit this land.'

"I believed but questions rose in my heart. I longed to see the promise fulfilled so I asked El Shaddai, 'How shall I know this?'

"Then the great God chose to 'cut' a covenant according to our custom. Yesterday I followed his instructions on that hill. Nearly all day I protected the covenant animals from preying birds. When the sun was nearly down a deep sleep fell on me. El Shaddai then said, 'Abram, your seed shall be as strangers in a land that is not theirs 400 seed times and harvests. Part of the time they shall serve in a foreign land but in the fourth generation they shall return here. Right now the iniquity of the Amorites is not full.'

"When the sun went down and it was dark a smoking furnace and a burning lamp passed between the divided animals and consumed them," he said joyfully. "Thus El Shaddai confirmed his fifth promise of a son and the inheritance of this land. Let's always choose to love, obey, and serve him. Then shall we know peace."

Afterward his people discussed their chieftain's words as they went to their tents. "Abram's whole life is bound up in producing a son," one man observed.

"But he's been listening to such promises for nearly 10 years," someone else protested.

"How can Sarai possibly have a child?" another demanded bluntly.

"She can't," a nearby woman said. "She's too old. They should adopt."

"But El Shaddai said not to," a voice interjected.

Eliezer, hearing the last remarks, said simply, "El Shaddai may be testing Abram."

The Request

When Hagar arrived at the sacrificial altar the evening shadows had crept across the hills. She laid Sarai's sitting mat next to hers then joined in the conversation of those already there. As now the chief overseer of the women she had gained great respect from Abram's people and felt a close bond to Sarai.

Tense and tired, Sarai arrived as Abram stood at the altar. After the sacrifice he spoke of his faith in El Shaddai. Once again Hagar noted the difference between the worship of El Shaddai and that of the Egyptian gods. She also had come to regard Abram as greater than Pharaoh the god-king. Even at his advanced age Abram could still inspire others. To watch his eyes and hear the ring in his strong voice as he spoke about the God he served clearly demonstrated that he knew El Shaddai well. More important, the patriarch made his whole tribe feel valuable to El Shaddai, to himself, and to themselves. Yet it seemed to Hagar the primary goal of Abram and Sarai—in fact, of their entire clan—centered around the birth of an heir. She wondered why.

As the people began to wander to their tents, Hagar and Sarai paused to watch the bats from the eastern caves flit across the full moon in the cloudless sky. But the sight of the moon triggered a mood in Hagar that she didn't understand. She turned to the silent woman by her side. "Sarai, how does the moon make you feel?"

"Just now? Lonely."

Hagar sensed her reluctance to talk. *Is she unhappy?* the girl wondered. *Why is Sarai so sad when she has no reason to be?* More and more Sarai's face wore a permanent look of anxiety.

Sarai's voice broke into her thoughts. "Come to my tent and braid my hair. The wind tangled it today."

"Good, I like braiding your hair. But you're so quiet. Are you sad?"

She thought a moment, then said, "I'll tell you about it while you braid."

In Sarai's tent they sat in the overlapped circles of light from three oil lamps. The burning wicks, steady and yellow, provided a dim but warm light. Hagar pulled the ivory comb through Sarai's long hair again and again. "Why do sparkles of light snap out of your hair?" the girl asked.

"I don't know. Hold the comb close to your arm without touching it."

Hagar ran the comb slowly above her outstretched arm. She laughed. "I feel prickles. What makes it?"

"It's a mystery. One of the countless unanswered questions in life. But the greatest of all fills my eyes with tears."

Her words roused a vague concern in Hagar. "I'll listen with my heart," she said gently.

Sarai choked back a sob. "I carry great shame. A cloud hangs over our marriage, because I've never produced a child."

Hagar finished one long braid. "Oh, Sarai, remember that El Shaddai has promised you and Abram a son."

"Ten years have passed since the first promise. But I only grow older."

"Maybe a son will come soon," the girl tried to assure her even as she felt her own eyes suddenly fill with tears.

When Hagar tied the braids and Sarai threw them back over her shoulders, the woman sighed. "Don't you find it strange that so long after being given a promise we still haven't received it?"

Hagar didn't know how to respond.

"Since El Shaddai doesn't want us to adopt Eliezer," Sarai continued, "it's up to me to give Abram an heir. A son would restore my dignity and establish my worth as his wife."

The girl leaned her head against Sarai's shoulder, then rose and went to a water jar, filled a clay cup, and handed it to her. "My lady must be patient."

Sarai drank and returned the cup. "I've often wondered if El Shaddai wants me to do something to obtain a son."

Hagar was puzzled as she sat beside her. "What could you do?"

Sarai wiped away her tears. "I've thought of following a Chaldean custom."

"What custom is that?"

"I can purchase a strong slave girl from the mountains of Subartu or Lullu. They make good substitute mothers."

Surprise and confusion mingled in the girl's face. "You mean Abram would have two wives and you wouldn't be the king-bearing wife?" she stammered.

"Not at all." Sarai laid her hand on Hagar's knee. "The custom is that I'd be present at his birth. The midwife would place him in my arms first. Then he'd be considered my son and I his mother."

Hagar silently considered the possibilities of the plan. She'd love to see Sarai and Abram with many children.

Sarai stared a long time at the girl, then continued, "You know Abram's descendants are to be kings." Suddenly the words tumbled out. "You're of royal blood—would you be the one to give us a son?" The words had barely left her mouth before she burst into sobs.

Hagar had never before seen the always dignified woman so upset. The girl sat in stunned silence while the magnitude of what Sarai had asked began to register. Memories of her life in the household of women in Egypt flashed before her. Then thoughts of Khuni raced through her heart. *Why is Baufra so far away? I need his counsel.*

Sarai touched her arm. As if reading Hagar's thoughts, she said, "You'd be free afterward to make a home of your own."

Hagar opened her mouth but no words came out. Her heart hammered against her ribs, its thumping bringing back memories of old sharp-eyed Seni. By contrast Abram, though also old in years, did not have wispy hair, a gray face drained of color, or a feebled walk. Instead, strong, courageous, and handsome, he enjoyed the status of a beloved leader among his people. He was a good and wise man. What woman would not dream of such a husband? The girl admired Sarai and would do anything to make her happy. Yet the request tore at Hagar's heart.

Feeling the pressure of a hand on her arm, she looked at Sarai's pleading eyes as they watched her. Time stood still as Sarai's gaze bored into her. Her mouth dry, Hagar swallowed and breathed hard to calm the inner storm raging inside her. In a voice as quiet as a leaf dropping, Hagar asked, "Why do you want me to do this?"

"Hagar, you're close to us, already part of the household. We love you. You love El Shaddai. Also you're a king's daughter. Will you honor us with a son?"

Still stunned, Hagar wondered if she were dreaming. She wanted Abram and Sarai to have children, longed for them to be happy. Many times she'd heard Abram say that choice is the structure upon which a person builds a life. Somehow she must make a momentous decision.

For the space of many heartbeats the two sat motionless. When Hagar lowered her head to her knees she felt Sarai stiffen. Her hands fretted nervously at the hem of her dress. They do deserve a son, she kept telling herself. Her voice trembled when she finally spoke. "My Mistress exalts me above my worth." Again silence stretched out. Breaking it against her will, Hagar whispered, "Sarai, I'll try to give you a son."

For a moment they looked at each other in quiet wonder, then their eyes filled with tears and they wept in each other's arms. Sarai kissed her on both cheeks and abruptly stood. "I'll see if Abram will go to your tent tonight."

▲ ▲ ▲

Suddenly aware that she was awake, Hagar opened her eyes. She was alone in her tent. For a long time she stared at the bare sleeping mat beside her, then rolled onto its emptiness and burst into grief-stricken tears. "I wish I could take back the promise," she choked out between great sobs. "But it's too late." Finally, exhausted, she listened to the rustle of the wind among the leaves. A gust caught the entry flap with a sharp crack and snapped it back and forth. Cold air crept beneath the edges of the tent and matched the chill in her heart.

"El Shaddai," she said aloud, "Your promise of a son to Abram has only brought me sorrow. Will it always be like this?"

Somehow she made herself go through the motions of everyday life. Vague thoughts haunted her. Was it her destiny to make kings and nations? "No," she forcefully reminded herself, "the child will be Sarai's."

Numbly she supervised the women's work. She saw their puzzled expressions and ignored their questioning glances. *Do they know what has happened?* she wondered. *That I have a secret too big for me to cope with?*

Later at her own tent a flurry of flour rose from her hands as she patted dough into flat disks and slapped them on the hot side of the clay oven. When they had baked she peeled them off and set them aside to cool. Next she threw cones from the previous year's stone pines on the embers. They opened with a pop, making it easier to extract the nuts.

The rest of the day she stayed away from people. That evening, her throat tight with tears, she sat huddled in the tent. She jumped almost in panic when Abram again entered.

The days went by slowly. Her nerves were constantly on edge. At times a sense of grief and of being trapped would overwhelm her and she would burst into tears. She would throw herself into some task so that she wouldn't have to think. *Were people watching her?* she wondered. *Do they know about Abram's nocturnal visits to her tent? That I am now his wife?* She lost interest in food and could not sleep. One day during rest period she walked out to her little herb garden. A startled lapwing with a wailing cry flapped past her face. It seemed to her then that her heart wanted to fly after the bird.

Sarai, always solicitous, approached her one afternoon. "Are you all right?" Her question rang with an undercurrent of hope.

The girl looked into her yearning eyes. For a long time a silent tension lay between them. Then Hagar flushed, mumbled, "I'm fine," and turned away.

Abram, on the other hand, remained remote and solemn yet she saw the questioning glances he flashed in her direction. She knew that she would forever feel guilty if she did not give him a son.

At last the day came when she knew that there was no turning back. She was with child.

With Child

Late that night Hagar stood in the entrance of her tent, trying to gather courage to tell Sarai. The camp was asleep though through the oaks she saw the glow of a shepherd's fire on a nearby hill. Wood smoke drifted in the night air. Lamplight spilled from Sarai's tent through an open flap. Hagar started toward it. At the edge of the light she saw Abram sitting cross-legged on a mat talking to Sarai. As the girl turned to leave, they spotted her and called her name.

She sat shy and afraid of the stillness. If only Sarai had been alone. They waited for her to speak. Finally, when Abram broke the silence, his voice sounded strange to her. "Hagar, are you with child?"

She could only stammer yes.

Their faces broke into smiles of joy, then came laughter clear like music on a cold morning. His excitement too great to contain, Abram slapped his knees and exclaimed, "Great is our God. El Shaddai has fulfilled His promise."

Sarai glanced at her husband. "We must take care of our child. Let's give Inara to Hagar as her personal servant."

The words they spoke and their happiness wrapped about the three of them, binding them together. A glow of joy began to warm Hagar's heart as she received their hugs and wishes for a peaceful night.

The following days transformed Hagar's life. News of the reason for Sarai and Abram's happiness traveled through the camp. Hagar noticed both men and women in small groups discussing the coming of the promised heir. She felt favored above all women.

One evening she sat alone before her tent, watching the embers in her fire die. All day she had kept busy forcing time forward. Now it stood frozen like a stone. "Stop it," she told herself, "he'll be here any minute."

"Hagar."

Startled, she glanced up. "Khuni, I saw you at the sacrifice and hoped you'd come." Relief flooded over her.

"I've been with Abram's caravan on a trading trip."

"So your dream of distant cities and trading expeditions came to pass."

"Yes, Abram let me take 10 donkey loads of my own along with his."

She started to tell him the news, then when the campfire flared for a second, she glimpsed in the yellow light a hurt expression on his drawn face. She bit her lip and lapsed into silence.

"Are you with child by Abram?" he suddenly blurted out.

The bitterness in his voice made her wince. For a time she didn't reply. He edged closer, watching her. Hurt sliced through her heart and trembled her voice. "Yes." She hesitated, then stammered defensively in Egyptian, "When he's born he will be Sarai's child."

Khuni paced back and forth. The cries of night birds pierced the air but he kept silent in both Amorite and Egyptian. She felt her heart ache and fought to hold back the tears.

"Why?" he demanded.

"To make Abram and Sarai happy."

"Did El Shaddai ask you to do it?"

She did not answer. Her heart thumped against her chest. "Did El Shaddai request this?" he repeated angrily. "I need to know."

"Sarai thought that El Shaddai wanted her to find a way."

Hagar would always remember his wounded cry, how he turned his face from her. His voice went on in the darkness. She heard his words but they made no sense to her. Bewildered and frightened, she realized that her relationship with Khuni had been shattered. *He's rejecting me, he's turning from me,* she thought to herself. Now that she was Abram's wife she could never be Khuni's.

He finally ran out of words and they both stood silently by the fire, equally awkward with each other. "Oh, Hagar." He put his arms around her and held her close. She felt his thudding heart until he gently pushed her from him. For a moment he hesitated, then turned away into the darkness.

For a long time she stared at where he had disappeared. An ember snapped and she jumped like a frightened deer. *Oh, Khuni, I've hurt you. If only I could change it back to the way we were before.*

Regret throbbed with each heartbeat. *I'm going to be a mother— no, Sarai's going to be a mother,* she reminded herself. She tried to picture the child. He would open his eyes and look up at Sarai. He would love her. Surely it would be a boy and resemble Abram.

In the morning she heard the sounds of the camp awakening to a new day. As she stretched her thoughts turned to the tiny life within her and she rolled out of bed. Things were different now. Inara came to ease the daily duties. "It's a beautiful morning. Hagar, how's Abram's heir?" *Not, how's your child?*

"He's been growing for nearly three months."

"You're greatly favored as his mother."

"Inara, how can I be his mother when he's to be given to Sarai?"

"You're his mother while he's inside you."

"If I could keep him, he'd love me as no other person has ever done."

"Better not think of it. Someday you'll have other children."

Later in the day Abram returned from trading with a passing caravan. Hagar and Sarai hastened to the tent to watch the men unload. As they watched Sarai squeezed Hagar's arm. "I count the days until I can see our son." Hagar winced at the words.

Abram walked over with a smile and handed Hagar a roll of rare purple linen dyed by the murex shell. "This is my first gift to our son."

The girl knew that by "our son" Abram meant his and Sarai's, but she thought to herself, *The child is his and mine.* She held the cloth close. "How beautiful." Rubbing her fingers over the fabric, she said to Sarai, "Feel it."

She noted a trace of sadness as Sarai touched the material, repeated "Beautiful," and turned away.

Every day she felt favored to be the mother of the promised son.

Soon she began to think of the life within her as *my child.* Questions whirled through her heart. *I want to give a real mother's love to this son. Why did El Shaddai give it to me and not Sarai?*

When Inara came in to trim the lamp wicks one evening, Hagar glanced up from the garment she stitched. "My son is kicking."

"Let me feel." The woman placed her hand on Hagar's abdomen. "He's strong."

"He's special, promised by El Shaddai, so he should be strong."

"I saw you letting Abram and Sarai feel the kicks."

"Abram always asks about his son. But I don't understand Sarai. She's changed."

Inara turned to look directly at Hagar. "It's hard for her to watch her husband pay attention to you."

"It's his son he's thinking about, not my comfort."

"Remember that—and be kind to Sarai."

Hagar gasped as old memories sparked new thoughts in her. Since infancy she had been raised among Pharaoh's wives and knew the prestige of the king-bearing wife. She was familiar with the plots and counterplots of the women in the royal household as they schemed for advantage and power. If she kept the child would she replace Sarai as chief wife? Was this what was bothering Sarai? "Inara, why do you think El Shaddai let me have the promised son instead of Sarai?"

The woman shrugged and looked uncomfortable. "It must be her age."

A thought flashed through Hagar's heart. *This life is growing in me and no one else. Can I make this child my own?* Out loud she said, "He is the jewel of my heart."

Inara shook her head. "Be careful, Hagar. Don't love him too much." When the servant woman had gone, Hagar stood at the threshold of her tent playing with a new idea. *Maybe El Shaddai doesn't want me to give up my child.*

Glancing up, she saw Sarai and another woman that she recognized as king Mamre's wife walking toward her. "Visit Hagar," she heard Sarai say to the visitor. "She oversees the women's work. Then later come back to my tent."

Feeling important, Hagar bore herself like royalty as she met Mamre's wife. "You honor my tent. Sit here in the shade."

The woman was tall and beautiful and wore shining crescents in her ears. Stray curls escaped from the black braids wound around her head and held in place by gold pins. Taking a seat, she remarked, "Sarai's camp is so clean and orderly."

"She likes cleanliness, and so do I. I'm Egyptian. We love beauty and order."

"Your bracelets are beautiful. Are they Egyptian?"

"They are. I brought them with me from Egypt."

"Sarai says that she and Abram have bestowed a great honor on you. Aren't you bearing them an heir?"

Hagar sat up straighter. "Yes, the son that El Shaddai has promised him, one who will be the father of kings."

"I have heard many good things about Abram's God."

"I wonder why El Shadddai lets me carry a child and not Sarai?" Hagar said without thinking.

The woman stared at her. "Isn't she too old?"

The girl thought a moment. "Maybe, but I wonder if there isn't another reason?"

Mamre's wife looked puzzled. "What do you mean?"

Hagar let her lips curl into a brief smile. "I wonder if she's really as nice as she appears."

The visitor's eyes widened with bewilderment. "I don't think that's possible," she said with disapproval and rose to leave. Hagar flushed and felt her pulse hasten.

That night, more tired than usual, Hagar sat at her tent door staring at the ground. Two camp watchmen passed by, a signal that it was late. A dry lump formed in her throat as anger, pity, guilt, and regret all battled in her heart. She tried to think of some way out of her predicament. Resentment on both Sarai's part and herself had begun to wedge them far apart, leaving their friendship balanced on a thin edge like that of a flint knife. How could she cast her child into the arms of her once best friend? She could see only a lifetime of regret if she gave up her son. Hot tears coursed down her face. *Sometimes I hate myself, but I want to keep my child, and besides, I'd be the mother of the promised son—the mother of kings.*

The anger in her voice startled her when she spoke aloud to the darkness, "I'll keep my baby. Wait and see."

The next morning Inara arrived extra early. "Hagar, you're up already? How's Sarai and Abram's son?"

"Abram's and my son."

The woman stared at her. "What do you mean?"

"Sarai is unkind."

"Aren't you judging without giving her a chance?"

"Why didn't El Shaddai give her a son. Her smooth lips must hide an evil heart."

Inara gasped then grew still as stone. Finally she stacked the sitting mats and broke the silence. "You promised the child to her. Are you exalting yourself above Sarai?"

Although guilt seized Hagar's heart she still protested, "But he is mine."

For some moments the two of them stood staring at each other. "Hagar, I'm your servant but I'm old enough to be your mother. I beg you to listen to me. Every moment we make decisions that will affect the rest of our lives, decisions that lead us either toward right or toward wrong. The choice you are about to make could bring you great unhappiness."

Hagar clenched her fists against her temples. "How could a mother of kings be unhappy?"

"Be loyal to your promise and you'll never regret it."

The words continued to echo in Hagar's heart all day. Nevertheless, she found additional opportunities to hint at her superiority over Sarai as the reason for her favored position. As time passed she increasingly boasted that she would be the mother of kings and nations. She would gloat over what she considered to be her own exalted position and downgrade Sarai's.

One afternoon after the rest period Hagar received an urgent summons to Sarai's tent. *Why would she send for me at this time of day?* she wondered as she started on her way. Walking was becoming more and more difficult as the child grew in her. The scent of brewed herbs from a pot on the bright embers outside wafted through the tent. She stared at Sarai's red-rimmed eyes and saw in them trouble and sorrow mingled. The woman indicated a mat and Hagar clumsily sat down. As she looked at Sarai, Hagar realized that for the first time she was afraid of her. Instead of a friend, the woman was a threat.

"Hagar, I've heard some disturbing gossip in the camp," Sarai said softly. "Do you know what I am referring to?"

Fear flooded the girl. "What gossip?" she asked, her voice trembling.

"It has been reported that you boast of your position. You claim to be favored above me. Do you think my heart is evil?"

"El Shaddai gave me the son—not you."

Sarai's mouth tightened, then she said, "You promised to produce a child for me. Now you want to keep it?" Her voice held suppressed anger.

"The child is mine," the girl shouted, staggering to her feet, ". . . and Abram's." She saw Sarai wince. "I intend to keep him. In Egypt the king-bearing mother doesn't give up her children."

"You are not in Egypt anymore," Sarai snapped, also standing.

Turning her back to Sarai, Hagar exploded, "The child is mine."

They edged away from each other. "Hagar, I must remove you as overseer of the women," Sarai said, barely suppressing her fury. "From now on you're just another servant."

For a second Hagar was stunned. Then she lunged at Sarai. "Abram will not let you treat the mother of his son this way," the girl screamed. "I will tell him."

Sarai pushed her away and with a frightening calmness, said, "Abram and I have discussed this. He told me you are in my care and that I am to do what I see best."

The words jolted Hagar. "But he's the father of my son . . ."

"He's my husband, and the baby will be mine."

Neither moved or said anything for several moments. Then Hagar rushed sobbing from Sarai's tent to her own.

Runaway

A lone in her tent and grief-stricken, Hagar lay on her mat and sobbed. "It's unfair," she wailed. "Sarai is unjust to reduce me from overseer to a mere servant. What will Khuni think? How will the rest of Abraham's people look at me?" Her tears scalded her cheeks. *Should I let Sarai have the child?* If possible, she cried even harder, unsure what to do.

"Why all the weeping?" Hagar raised her head and saw Inara holding the tent flap aside. "It is time for the sacrifice."

"Go away," Hagar shouted.

Inara knelt and gently touched her shoulder. "Hagar, your tears speak of a broken and crushed heart. What happened? Have your lips betrayed you?"

The girl pushed herself up and wiped at her tears with the backs of her hands. "Sarai says things that make me swell up seven times in anger. Their injustice stings my heart."

"Why do you try to take Sarai's place?"

"I am the king-bearer."

Tears filled Inara's dark eyes as she said, "Are you saying that Sarai is an obstacle in your way?"

Hagar rolled away from Inara's hand. Fresh tears fell as she replied, "Sarai is . . . she took away my status in camp. I just won't let Sarai brand me as a slave."

Inara stood. "Hagar, your lips have been set against Sarai. Your tongue boasts of your favored position. What do you expect? I'm older than you, so I must speak. You need to understand Sarai. You honored her request to bear the child for her. Why have you changed?"

The woman's words cut through Hagar's heart like an obsidian knife. For a moment she reproached herself for claiming the child. Then, with a shudder, she declared, "I will be a mother of nations. My name will be remembered and never forgotten. El Shaddai gave me the child, and I intend to keep it." She hesitated. "From now on I'll stay in my tent."

Inara's hands dropped. "As you like."

When Hagar's sobs at last subsided her lungs felt raw. Her thoughts leaped and twisted. *In Egypt I lived in the royal household with access to the palace. Here I live in a goat-hair tent. In Egypt servants attended me. Now I am a servant myself. Long ago I walked along the life-giving Nile but now I climb rock-strewn hills. In Egypt I dressed in linen, now I dress in scratchy wool. By the Nile I ate fancy food in fine dishes, now plain food in crude pottery. In Egypt I may have an elegant tomb, here only a burial jar, a sheepskin, and a cave. There I walked in formal gardens, while now I struggle through tangled brush and grass. In Egypt I worshiped visible gods but here an unseen God. I left behind the quarrels, schemes, and plots of the household of women for what I thought was peace and love among Sarai's people. Now it's lost.* For a long time her heart was silent and empty. Then a new idea began to take shape in it. *Somehow I'll keep the child from Sarai and will become the mother of kings.*

She remembered the welcome Sinuhe had received when he returned to Egypt. *Would I be welcome in Egypt if I came back bearing a young heir? He should grow up in the palace and receive the training for one destined to be a father of kings.* Yes, she would go back to Egypt and again look upon the moonlit calm of the Nile. *No,* she convinced herself, *I don't want to spend the rest of my life with an ancient man and his bedraggled sheep.*

Hagar squirmed on her side and lifted the edge of the tent. Across the camp the smoldering cooking fires wafted their pungent smoke through the air. Scrambling to her feet, she wrapped sleeping skins around dried raisins, figs, flour, some flat barley loaves, and three extra waterskins.

After slinging the roll on her shoulder, she slipped from the tent and headed south away from the feeble light of the fire. She tried to avoid stepping on rocks and making noise. When she reached the donkey stockade she hid the roll in the brush. Then she walked through the night shadows of the oaks back to her tent. The moon hadn't risen yet but the starlight served her better. She would wait in her tent until the camp had gone to sleep.

Inara paused outside Hagar's tent and called her name but the girl didn't respond and the woman left. For a moment a wave of loneliness swept over Hagar but she fought it back. Next she packed clothes, jewelry, and pieces of silver into two large baskets. Silver was more valuable than gold in Egypt since the country had no silver deposits. Finally she tied a bag of smooth stones and a sling around her waist.

At last the moment came when the moon poked above the trees on the eastern hills. The only noise from the sleeping camp was that of the voices of the night insects. Then darting from shadow to shadow she headed along the trail to the donkey stockade. There she strapped her baggage to the back of one and her water skins to another.

After listening for some sound that indicated the location of the night watchmen and concluding they were nowhere nearby, she eased the donkeys out of the stockade and down the trail toward Beersheba. When dawn vanished the night over the western hills she sought a secluded spot in the trees near the trail. After eating some bread and raisins she closed her eyes.

Late in the day she awoke. The endless series of forking paths confused her. Somehow she had to keep to the most traveled trail. It led down from the hills of Hebron to the desert of Beersheba.

The next day a north wind brought her the sounds of an approaching caravan. She turned off the trail and waited to see if it was one she wanted to join. When they drew near she saw that it was a small caravan consisting of several families. Returning to the trail she waited beside the donkeys. The caravaneers appraised and discussed her among themselves as they approached.

"Are you going to Egypt?" Hagar asked.

"No, En-mishpat," a burly man answered in Amorite, not trying to hide his great curiosity at seeing a young woman traveling alone.

A tall woman on a camel asked, "Are you Egyptian?"

Hearing her native tongue and sensing her good fortune, Hagar replied, "Yes, I'm going home."

"Alone?"

"Yes."

The woman studied her. People did not travel by themselves, especially women. It was too dangerous. "Join us," she said, making a decision. "You can pick up a caravan to Egypt at En-Mishpat." The woman pointed. "Ride behind my donkeys."

"You are kind. I'll go with you." And Hagar slipped into the place indicated.

The caravan traveled fast, but Hagar managed to keep up with them. But her heart struggled with thoughts both of the home she was leaving and the one to which she was returning. She looked forward to seeing the glint of Amon Re on the Nile, the clean rooms of the royal palace, and scents of familiar spices and perfumes. But then uncertainty about her welcome in Egypt nagged at her heart. Would Pharaoh agree to train a child destined to be the father of many nations? At times doubt would trouble her. Other times she had to seal her heart against the onslaught of homesickness for her life in Abram's tent.

Three days later the caravan came to a spring and decided to rest for a day. Here Hagar parted company. She'd remain behind and wait for another caravan. The closer she approached the open desert the more confused became her feelings. They seemed to shift and roll with the wind.

After the caravan had vanished Hagar felt intensely alone. Her emotions blurred together in a flood of doubt and pain. Had her running away destroyed any chance for happiness? *Baufra always said, "Love has a way of making problems for itself,"* she thought to herself. *Is that why my relationship with Sarai is in shambles.*

She sat by the well with her head in her arms. *I don't understand the misery inside myself. Abram says that El Shaddai understands us and knows our thoughts. I wonder.*

Hagar poured out a prayer to El Shaddai. "If you can hear, help me." A shock ran through her as though lightning had touched her. With an effort she forced herself to stand. Did she hear someone?

She glanced toward the spring but saw that she was totally alone. Then she heard it again.

"Hagar, servant of Sarai, where have you come from, and where are you going?" a voice asked.

She spoke to the emptiness around her. "I'm running away from my mistress Sarai." Why had she revealed that? Then she saw him and was afraid.

"I am an angel of El Shaddai," the stranger announced. "Go back to your mistress and submit to her." Then the being added, "I will so increase your descendants that they will be too numerous to count."

Speechless, Hagar stared at the angel. "You are now with child and you will have a son," he said. "You shall name him Ishmael for the Lord has heard of your misery."

He isn't telling me to give my son to Sarai, she thought to herself.

"He will be a wild donkey of a man; his hand will be against everyone and everyone's hand against him, and he will live in hostility toward all his brothers."

Amazed that she had seen the angel and survived, she said, "You are the God who sees me. This place is sacred because the invisible God appeared here." Somehow she knew without making a conscious decision that she would return to Abram's camp with his son. Her feet turned north.

Hagar's Return

𐃘𐃘𐃘𐃘𐃘𐃘𐃘𐃘𐃘𐃘𐃘𐃘𐃘𐃘𐃘𐃘𐃘𐃘𐃘𐃘𐃘𐃘𐃘𐃘𐃘𐃘𐃘𐃘𐃘𐃘

Alone in her tent, Hagar listened to the laughter around the evening fires and rubbed her nose as an occasional breeze brought her the pungent smell of smoke. She felt confident that no one had seen her return but the guards might notice the travel-worn donkeys back in the corral.

A cloud of sadness enveloped her and she wiped away tears. She felt as if trapped between two worlds and belonging to neither. Sometimes she thought like an Egyptian, other times like the Sand-dwellers she had joined.

My name has great value to me, she told herself. *It must live through my son.* The idea dominated her whole being. That was the Egyptian in her.

Hagar jumped to her feet as the sounds of voices and footsteps warned her that the families were returning to their tents. *What shall I do? Go to Abram and Sarai now or in the morning?* Her heart leaped into her throat as someone fumbled with the ties on her tent flap. She buried herself under some sheepskins in the darkest corner just as Inara entered.

Holding a lamp high, Inara inspected the interior. Then her eyes riveted on the corner where Hagar hid beneath the skins. She could see the outline of the girl's body. Inara took a few steps toward her. "Hagar?"

The girl rose to her feet. "Inara."

Setting the lamp down, the woman rushed to embrace her. Their mingled tears spoke the words of their hearts.

"Hagar," Inara said gently, "Abram has offered many prayers to El Shaddai for the safe return of his son."

The girl held her breath. ""Did Sarai?"

"All the camp prayed. There will be great rejoicing over your return."

Bursting into tears, Hagar began to sob, "I'm sorry, I'm sorry . . ."

"I have come here every day looking for you. I'm glad you are back."

Hagar's tears streamed down her face. "I missed you too, and the whole camp."

Inara took her hand. "El Shaddai protected you."

"I know. El Shaddai sent an angel to talk to me."

The woman gasped. "He sent an angel to you? Why?"

"He told me to return here."

"An angel talked to you! Did you tell Abram?"

"I have seen no one except you. Oh, Inara, I've wondered—should I tell him tonight?"

The woman nodded.

"I'm afraid."

"I will accompany you." Inara hesitated. "Unless you want to go alone."

Hagar grasped the woman's hands. "No, please go with me."

"Do you want to go to Sarai or Abram's tent?"

"Abram's."

"I'll find out if he will see you, then return."

"I'll be ready."

Removing her travel-worn clothes, Hagar washed her face, arms, and feet. The fresh garments provided a speck of confidence. When Inara returned Hagar asked, "What did he say?"

"He thanked El Shaddai for the answer to his prayers. Then he sent for Sarai. They will be waiting in his tent."

Darkness shrouded the camp but she followed Inara and her lamp. Ahead she saw Abram and Sarai waiting. When they came close she could see their anxious faces in the flickering light of Sarai's lamp. The couple pulled her inside the well-lighted tent. "Hagar, we are glad you're safe," Abram said.

Speechless, the girl turned to look at Sarai who still held her arm. A thin, confused smile struggled to form on her lips as the woman said, "Welcome home, Hagar."

After they settled on rugs around the fire in the brazier Abram asked in a voice gentle yet firm, "What's this all about, Hagar?"

She glanced at Sarai, remembering the hurt and anger she had seen in her eyes. Now Hagar noticed only a quiet sadness. Yet it was hard for the girl to speak and her voice trembled, "Sarai took away my status and honor. She said I could no longer oversee the women. Because of the shame I ran away. I thought my son could be trained in Egypt to be a real king."

"But I sent men along the way to Egypt looking for you." Abram interrupted.

"I hid from them, my Lord."

"You've been gone almost a whole moon. How far did you go?"

"To the well between Kadesh and Bered. I call the well, Beer Lahai Roi. I separated from a caravan there. While I was deciding what to do next, El Shaddai sent an angel to talk to me."

"He sent an angel?" Abram burst forth excitedly. "Are you sure?" Hagar felt he questioned her honesty.

"Yes, an angel spoke to me." She fell silent, exhausted by conflicting emotions.

As Abram studied her a look of amazement spread over his face. A long silence crept into the tent. "Tell us what the angel told you," he said finally.

Hagar glanced at Inara, seeking help, but the woman remained quiet, watching her closely. The girl fought to control her voice. "The angel instructed me to return and obey Sarai. He said I'll have a son and my descendants will be too numerous to count."

"But they'll be Abram's descendants," Sarai interrupted, a sharp edge of bitterness in her voice.

Abram gazed quietly at Hagar for some time. The shadow of some emotion she saw in his eyes now frightened her. A cloud of sadness descended upon the tent.

A baby cried in a nearby tent. Then Abram spoke, gentleness and sympathy in his words. "Hagar, tell us all that the angel told you."

She closed her eyes and remembered. "He said we are to name him Ishmael."

Without hesitation Abram said, "Ishmael it will be. Truly this is the promised son." Then he stood and in a voice ringing with authority, "Return to your tent. Be sure we see you early in the morning."

As she left Hagar whispered, "Because El Shaddai spoke to me through His angel, I'll not run away again."

Ishmael's Birth

When Hagar stretched and turned over her unborn child responded with strong kicks. She placed her hand over her rounded stomach and laughed while the kicking continued. "Your heart that beats in me will still beat after I'm dead and placed in a cave. My name will live on in you, Abram's son. When I'm nothing, you'll still walk about in the heat of the sun. You'll breathe and beget thrones and kingships."

Hagar met Abram and Sarai in Sarai's tent where the woman sat silently on a rug, her feet crossed at the ankles. Hagar glanced at the self-possessed and masterful woman whom Abram loved and felt a twinge of jealousy mixed with perverse delight at Sarai's childlessness. Pausing only long enough to gain control of her voice, she said, "Lord and Mistress, I've come at your bidding." Then without thinking, she added, "I come as the one El Shaddai chose to bear your heir."

She saw a flicker of annoyance in his eyes and her blood burned in her face. Abram turned to pick up some items from a low table. "Hagar, Sarai and I welcome you and our son back. El Shaddai answered our prayers for your safe return."

Sarai moved uneasily but managed to smile. "We have some gifts for you, Hagar."

Abram held them out. "Here's a bracelet for your arm, sandals for your feet, and a bolt of fine cloth for the child."

"Thank you, my Lord."

He frowned. "You know that we speak as equals in this camp."

Measuring each word, Sarai announced, "Hagar, your position as overseer of the women will be restored to you." As Sarai paused again, Hagar felt a whirlwind of gladness sweep through her heart. "The position is yours only if you are loyal," Sarai resumed. "Do not gossip and conjecture about our son and his parents to others."

There it was again—"our son"—as though the child was theirs and not hers. A hot answer sprang up in her but she choked it back. Silence must be her strength and security.

Abram sat down. "You may go, Hagar. See Eliezer for new instructions."

Hagar left knowing Abram and his wife would spend long hours discussing her. She vowed that she'd make Sarai eat one by one the words that she had used to poison his heart against her.

Inara met her at her tent. "Hagar, while you were away Khuni and Meret announced they'll marry soon."

Hagar's heart stopped. "I knew they'd marry someday," she finally stammered.

"Khuni found a female child abandoned along the caravan route. He saved the child and gave her to Meret. She's raising the girl as a personal servant."

"I'm glad for Meret. When my time comes I want to go to her mother. She's a good midwife. Ishmael can be born in her tent. Promise you won't call Sarai or Abram until after the birth so that Sarai can't be the first to hold my son—or he'll be hers."

"That's not right."

"This child's mine, not Sarai's," Hagar insisted.

Inara shook her head. "Hagar, you once loved Sarai, yet now your hate is stronger than if you had never loved."

The girl stared at her but did not reply.

In the days that followed Hagar hummed over her work either to the child or to herself. The women readily accepted her supervision, but she had to avoid their questioning. Often she caught Sarai watching her. At other times Hagar sensed the woman's disapproval when she let Abram feel his son's strong movements.

By now she felt heavy and awkward as she and Inara returned from searching for herbs in the scrubby woods. When they stopped to rest, Hagar said, "Look at the dark clouds to the southwest."

"We'd better start for the tents."

147

Although the wind eased the day's heat, Hagar groaned. "A storm's coming. See the sheep all stand with their tails to the wind."

Once in camp Hagar felt a mild pain slice across her midsection and grip its way around to her lower back. She handed the herbs to Inara. "My time's come. Meet me at the birthing tent."

"I'll put these in the tent, then I'm going with you."

Staggering, Hagar reached the birthing tent. Inara went for Meret and her mother. When Hagar's eyes became accustomed to the dark interior she saw two stones at the back of the tent. Sheep skins covered the stones and old but soft rags were on the ground between them. Meret and her mother came with lighted lamps and started a fire in the brazier. The tent shuddered from a gust of wind and scattered rain sounded a tattoo on the roof and sides.

The midwife ran her hands over Hagar's stomach. "The child's position is right. You'll soon have your son." She led her to the birthing stones. A heavy ache in the small of Hagar's back made it hurt to move, but she knew that she must. She clenched her fists and moaned.

Sitting on the stones Hagar felt a momentary glow of pleasure as she remembered that the midwife had referred to the child as "your son." *At least someone recognizes him as mine,* she thought.

Hagar felt perspiration trickle down her forehead and gripped the stones as a contraction stabbed at her then fled. Pain after pain shot through her, leaving her gasping for breath. Another wrenching pain and Hagar stifled a scream. Dimly she heard the midwife instructing her. "Take a deep breath—push." She fought against the dizziness and nausea but sank into darkness. Finally, in a rush of water, the head emerged. "Push, push, the child's coming," the midwife shouted. Kneeling, she received the child and held it upside down to clean mucus out of its mouth. Ishmael struggled to fill his lungs with air and his angry cry rang through the tent.

Tears of relief and joy filled Hagar's eyes and sobs of triumph and thankfulness tore at her heart. When Meret placed Ishmael in her arms she pressed her mouth against his damp cheek. *I give you my life and heart,* she thought as she held the infant a long time. "Go tell Abram that he has a son," she told Inara at last.

Meret took the child and held him while her mother severed the cord with an obsidian knife. Then she bathed him in olive oil and salt.

When the afterbirth had come, the midwife helped Hagar lie down. Tired beyond reason, she dozed.

Meret handed Ishmael to her mother and hurried to lift the tent flap to Abram's excited voice. His drenched presence filled the tent. With a joyful laugh he reached for Ishmael. "It's a son." In the flickering light Hagar watched him inspect the newborn and hoped the child would grow to be like his father. She saw the tenderness in Abram's eyes as the furrows in his brow deepened. Holding Ishmael close, he said, "My firstborn is so strong. He's perfect. El Shaddai is good to give me this lad."

Then Abram turned to her. "Are you all right?"

She nodded, unable to speak but overjoyed that Abram approved of his son. All she wanted to do now was to sleep.

The blare of ram's horns shattered the quiet of the damp night to announce the birth of Abram's son—the father of kings according to El Shaddai's promise.

Hagar and the Child Ishmael

The rains of five winters had fallen and any day Abram would take more control of his son. Hagar hugged the boy close and kissed the top of his head. "When you sleep in your father's tent, will you come back to mine every day?" she asked him

"Yes, I'll eat with you."

"Good. You're to visit the shepherds today."

They finished eating just as Abram with several servants and donkeys arrived for Ishmael. Abram helped his son climb onto a donkey and turned to Hagar. "We're visiting a nearby camp." He scanned the sky. "The weather's been unusually warm. It could mean a storm."

As the day wore on Hagar watched clouds darken the sky. Gray and purple with churning edges, they piled up on one another. The procession of clouds kept moving across the sky. The camp took on a drab and gray cast. The women had stopped their grinding of flour and taken the spinning and weaving into the tents. Girls picked up old woolen cloaks spread with drying herbs and carried them into shelter. Eliezer hurried by. "Hagar, tell the women to get the children under shelter."

Before Hagar could obey the shepherds sounded an alarm on their flutes. Women and children disappeared into their tents. Abram strode up, carrying his son on his back, and eased him to the ground. "Here, Hagar, care for Ishmael," and he hurried away.

Hagar reached for the child's hand. "Come." Lightning sliced the sky and thunder rumbled through the camp.

Ishmael pulled away, screaming, "My frog!" He turned over a

150

small basket and grabbed the frog in both hands. Hagar pushed him into her tent.

More lightning ripped the sky and lashed downward. Rain slanted down and the wind intensified. The tent groaned and swayed.

Ishmael, concerned for the frog, placed it in a basket and covered it with wool. He looked up at Hagar. "Mother, it's afraid."

Taking her son by the hand, she said, "Let's watch the storm." She pulled back the flap. "Look, Ishmael, El Shaddai hurls strange rain to the ground."

It fell in round hard crystals the size of bird's eggs and thudded a tattoo on the tent. Quickly the storm moved east, leaving a blanket of white on the ground. Hagar, Ishmael, and others rushed to investigate the marvel but the sun melted the stones-of-heaven before their eyes.

Meret emerged from behind the tent. "Hagar, come with me. I need more herbs for drying."

"I need some too." She left Ishmael with Inara and went with Meret into the woods. Leaves and branches carpeted the ground, and the hail had smashed the herbs. "Meret, I don't understand why El Shaddai brings forth green plants and then lets them die this way."

"Khuni says it's because sin came into the world. Abram explained it to him."

"Well, let's find all we can. We'll need to harvest the parsley in our gardens too."

Meret shook beads of water from the broken herbs. "I like to be in the woods after a rain. The wet earth smells so clean and fresh."

"I do too. I like the smell of wet grass. I don't even care that these dripping leaves are soaking my clothes."

"Makare and Shepant will soon be old enough to help gather herbs. Right now they like to play and are waiting for Khuni to bring them kittens from Egypt. Maybe there'll be one for Ishmael."

"I hope so. I think Ishmael would like one. Meret, you're lucky."

"Why?"

"You married Khuni and have two children, and I have only Ishmael."

"Doesn't Abram want more?"

"He never says so and neither does Sarai."

"Have you talked with them about having more?"

"No, but Ishmael needs a brother."

"Why don't you ask Abram?"

"I think I will."

The next morning Ishmael stretched on his mother's bed, chattering to Hagar who was half asleep. "Mother," he shook her shoulder, "was my frog afraid?"

She jerked awake. "Why do you ask? Is someone bothering it?" Abram's people did not hold frogs in the high regard that Egypt did.

"No, I mean when fire came from the sky and the clouds roared."

"What made you think it was afraid?"

"It's legs jerked every time fire came."

"It was a big storm. Ask your father if it was afraid. Come, we must eat before he arrives for you."

That night, which was cooler than usual, Abram didn't bring Ishmael back to her tent. As Hagar lay in her bed of skins she wondered if Ishmael was cold. Surely Abram would properly care for him. She pictured the shepherds in thick woolen cloaks crouching around their fires. Ishmael must be asleep, warm and cozy in a tent or cave.

She mused about his day. Did he watch the lop-eared goats leap upon the rocks? Did he see them rearup against the twisted trunks and tear at the branches of the old olive trees? Did he listen to the shepherds blow their plaintive music to summon the sheep? Hagar fell asleep.

Late the next day Abram walked into camp carrying a newborn lamb. Ishmael, his garment torn by thorns, tagged along wearing a happy smile. "Mother, I get to care for the lamb."

Hagar knelt and hugged him close. "I missed you." She looked over his head at Abram.

"One of the ewes lambed late. She had three and not enough milk for all. Ishmael fell in love with this one."

She petted the lamb. "It's a beauty."

"I've asked a servant to build a small brush pen. He'll bring sheep's milk for it."

"Fine. I'll help him."

"Don't help him too much, Hagar. Let him solve any problems that might come up with its care. That's part of Ishmael's education. After a time we'll take the lamb back to the shepherds."

During the following days Hagar watched Ishmael's tenderness with the lamb. When he had first used her comb in his hair and held it close to his arm the hair stood up and crackled. He had rolled on the tent floor and giggled. Now he discovered that the comb couldn't penetrate the lamb's wool. But when he rubbed it back and forth on the lamb, it produced the same effect on his arm as when he combed his own hair. Hagar enjoyed watching him share such discoveries with his friends.

Day by day she sought to approach Abram with her request before he took Ishmael and the lamb back to the shepherds. "If I had another child I'd not be lonely when Ishmael's gone," she told herself. It must become a reality.

One night her chance came. She saw Abram tarry at the fire to talk to his guest, a roving storyteller, who had entertained them around the fire. The other children followed their parents, but Ishmael ran back to sit beside her. Together they watched the flames ripple over the embers. Moths, attracted to the fire, darted toward it and then flew away from the heat.

Hagar saw Abram come out of the shadows toward them. "Inara, go on back to your tent. I want to speak to Abram." She stood as he picked up Ishmael and kissed him three times, once on each cheek and once on the boy's brow.

"Hagar, are you waiting to see me?"

The gathering darkness brought a measure of control to the struggle in her heart. "Yes, I need to talk to you." They moved apart so Ishmael could walk between them.

When they neared her tent, Ishmael ran ahead to check on his lamb and Abram sat on a boulder. Hagar turned to the boy's father. "Abram, Ishmael needs brothers and sisters."

Startled, Abram jumped to his feet. He was close enough that even in the dim light she could see his stricken face trying to compose itself. "No!"

"I should have another child by now."

He looked into her face. "We only agreed on one."

"What if Ishmael should die? You'd have no heir."

"He's El Shaddai's promised one and God will care for him. Hagar, if you had wanted more children you'd have given Ishmael to Sarai."

"El Shaddai didn't ask me to part with him." Her voice broke in her rage and she covered her face with her hands.

Just then they looked down and saw Ishmael standing close and glancing from one to the other with large moist eyes. He turned aside as if to hide his tears. Picking him up, Abram held him close to his chest. "El Shaddai promised you to me. He loves you."

Abram sat his son down and turned to Hagar. "Let's not mention again what can't come to pass." Then he turned toward his tent.

She knew he'd go to Sarai. Why did Sarai have all his love? Hagar continued to brood over Abram's unwillingness to give her more children. Later, perhaps, she'd approach him again.

A few days later she saw Ishmael offer Sarai a handful of wild flowers. The woman smiled and started to accept them until she saw Hagar watching. Her smile disappeared and she abruptly refused the flowers.

Crying, Ishmael ran to his mother. "Sarai won't take the flowers I picked for her."

Hagar knew that she should have comforted him but her anger against Sarai overwhelmed her. "Ishmael, you must learn to stay away from Sarai. She doesn't like us and she is not good for you." From that day on the boy began to avoid Abraham's wife.

When Ishmael was 12 Abram moved him to a tent of his own. Then his father placed him under Eliezer's training. Soon the chief servant took the lad on an extended trip to gather henna and wild honey for the next caravan to Egypt.

Ismael became skilled with the sling and spear. He learned to play tunes on his shepherd's flute. However, most of all, he liked to practice archery and roam the woods.

Hagar's pride in Ishmael grew daily. They smiled at each other across the fire. She and the camp knew the inheritance was in the palm of Ishmael's hand and hers, too, for she would be the heir's mother. Her heart at last was content. And now that Ishmael was almost totally under Abram's control, Sarai was also friendlier.

An idea began to grow in Hagar's mind. In the royal palace in Egypt everyone borrowed, lent, bought, or sold favors. She'd heap favors on Sarai and Abram until they'd have to repay her. Clasping her hands around her knees, she swayed back and forth as she thought out what she would do. "A plan has come into my heart that should bring Ishmael brothers and sisters," she said to Inara who was mending a garment.

The woman's bone needle paused in the air. "Hagar, don't go astray in your heart."

"Watch me, Inara."

During the following moons Hagar gave Sarai and Abram extra help, cooked special dishes, ran extra errands, or played her harp just for their enjoyment. Once she overheard Sarai comment to Abram that "Hagar's becoming more like the girl we brought back from Egypt." Somehow the remark pleased Hagar.

Early one morning she spotted Abram walking down the trail from the hilltop where he talked to El Shaddai. Turning to Inara, she said, "Finish baking this bread. I must speak to Abram."

As she slowly approached him she went over the words she'd say. When they met, Abram said, "Hagar, you've something on your heart."

Her gaze met his. "Did El Shaddai talk to you?"

"No, I talked to Him."

"One day He'll talk to you again, then you'll tell us His words."

"Hagar, you've changed. Sarai and I have noticed."

"We've all changed. Could it be otherwise in 13 years?"

Abram smiled. "What's in your heart Hagar?"

"I'm ready to give Ishmael his just due—brothers and sisters," she said slowly, softly.

Abram stepped backward and closed his eyes. It was as though he had received a blow beneath the heart. When he recovered he spoke in a low, kind voice. "I'll not wound Sarai's heart again."

Hagar laughed and it caught like a sob in her throat. "One love need not drive out another love."

He reached for her arm. "I respect you as Ishmael's mother. You've given me a wonderful son. I would like many more like him—but it can't be. It was never intended that I give you more children. I can't be a real husband to you."

Flushed and ready to weep, she stammered at him, "It's unjust. I wonder what it would be like to have a real husband all my own." She turned and fled to her tent.

"Why the tears?" Inara asked when she entered.

"Abram won't give me more children. It's all because of Sarai."

Inara shook her head. "Don't harden your heart against Sarai. Remain friends with her, and it will pay off in time."

When Ishmael had almost reached 13 and Abram almost 100, El Shaddai once again appeared to the patriarch. Abram repeated the words of his God at the evening fire. "El Shaddai said to me, 'I'm changing your name to Abraham, for you will be the father of many nations.

"'Make a covenant with me. Circumcise every male in your household, even the eight-day-old child. The circumcision shall be an everlasting covenant between us from generation to generation. As for Sarai your wife, call her Sarah. I'll bless her. She'll be mother of nations, kings, and people.'"

Abram shook his head in disbelief. "I must confess that when I heard this I fell on my face and laughed. I said quietly in my heart, 'Shall a child be born to me when I am 100 years old? Shall Sarah, almost 90 years old, bear a child?'"

Can it be the promises have started again? Hagar thought. *Isn't Ishmael enough for Abram or El Shaddai?* She glanced at those around her. No one showed surprise except Eliezer who hung on to Abraham's every word. *Abram's getting old,* she told herself. *He's mingling the old promises with what he thinks is a new revelation.*

Then Abram's next words seized her attention. "I prayed for Ishmael that he might live before El Shaddai as the promised seed. But El Shaddai said, 'Sarah, your wife, shall bear a child at a set time next year. Because you laughed you will name him Isaac (he laughs).'"

A feeling of desperation started deep within Hagar and rushed to the surface. *Surely what Abram said couldn't be true. Would Ishmael be safe if Sarai did have a child of her own?*

Three Strangers

ⅢⅢⅢⅢⅢⅢⅢⅢⅢⅢⅢⅢⅢⅢⅢⅢⅢⅢⅢⅢⅢⅢⅢⅢⅢⅢⅢ

All morning it was hot and dry. Unseasonable temperatures turned Mamre into a smelter's furnace. Men and women sat panting in the scant shade of their tents. Hagar glanced at Inara sipping water and groaned. "How long can we endure such heat?"

Pouring water in her cupped hand, Inara wiped her face and wrists. "This too will pass," she said simply, then glanced at Hagar. "Where's Ishmael?"

"Abraham sent him with Eliezer's sons to give the shepherds extra help. I hope he's sitting in the shade of a cool cave playing his flute to calm the sheep."

Inara rose and retreated farther into the shade. "The shepherds have been running out of pasture because of the poor winter rains but this heat makes matters even worse."

Hagar dropped to her bed. The dust that rose from her mat made her want to sneeze. "Inara, let's shake the dust out of the mats."

"Can't it wait until evening?"

"No. Now. It won't take long."

Even after they shook the mats the smell of dust remained. "Inara, hang them on the ropes around the tent. Perhaps that will help."

As the woman started outside, she pointed. "Look, Abraham's sitting at the door of his tent staring out over the plain."

"So?" Hagar turned her gaze to see what seemed to fascinate Abraham and saw not far away three strangers. The patriarch rose and ran to meet them. She and Inara quietly watched.

When Abraham bowed to the strangers Hagar heard him say, "My Lord, may I find favor in your sight. Please stay a while with your servant." She did not catch their reply but heard Abraham continue, "Let me bring water to wash your feet that you may rest from the heat under this tree."

When the men were seated in the shade, Abraham suggested, "Let me bring a morsel of bread to refresh you, then you may continue your journey."

"Very well, do as you say," one visitor nodded.

Abraham briefly entered Sarah's tent, then while a servant washed the guests' feet he hastened to a nearby herd. Sarah emerged from her tent and, standing behind the strangers, beckoned to Hagar and Inara. They dropped the bedding and hurried to her. "Abraham wants three measures of flour baked for our guests. Bake the bread on your hearth stones and bring the loaves here."

They forgot the heat in the excitement of guests. While Inara collected a bowl and flour Hagar stirred up the cooking fire that had become a pile of pale ashes. She saw Abraham return with a young calf. He gave it to a young man, saying, "Dress it well for these important guests."

"These visitors seem different," Inara said, kneading the dough.

"I sense it too, Inara." Hagar scrubbed at the baking stones. "We must keep as much sand out of the cakes as possible, then Sarah will be happy." She slapped dough on the hot stones. "I hope they have brought many tales of far away places to share with us." In a short time the aroma of baking bread permeated the still air.

Inara snatched a loaf of bread and juggled it between her hands until it cooled enough to hold. "You and Sarah are getting along better, and I'm glad."

"My relationship with her has had its ups and downs since Ishmael's birth. It's improving, especially since Sarah likes my son better all the time." Hagar patted dough on the hot stone. "Whenever I feel angry toward her I remember the hard words that passed between us. The pain of remembering is great."

Hagar and Inara, their faces reddened by the baking fire, carried stacks of bread to Sarah who was pouring milk curds into large cups. Hagar stacked the bread on one of the best clay platters. "Will the men have news and tales to share at the fire tonight?"

Sarah threw her braids tied with strips of cloth over her shoulders. "I hope so. The men must be important among their people."

"But where are their servants, camels, and donkeys?" Inara asked. "How could they travel without them?"

Sarah placed the bread and curds on a low table by the entrance. "I've wondered that too. Perhaps they left them some place along the way."

Abraham picked up the prepared food and returned to his guests. The young servant brought the roasted calf and Abraham set everything before the men. He stood nearby, talking to them while they ate.

Sarah, Hagar, and Inara settled on a rug to watch and listen through the open tent door. One guest in a commanding voice asked, "Where is Sarah your wife?"

From where Hagar was sitting she could see the puzzled expression on Abraham's face as he replied, "She's in the tent."

"I'll return to you in due season, because Sarah your wife shall have a son."

Startled, Sarah rocked back on her heels. Her eyes couldn't have been wider or more unbelieving than if she had seen the firmament torn apart. Hagar thought that she must be laughing at the idea within her heart.

Leaning toward the other two women, Sarah whispered, "Do you really think that I'll have a son when I'm this old, and with Abram old also?"

The stranger's next words caught their attention. "Why did Sarah laugh, saying, 'Shall I bear a child when I'm old?' Is anything too hard for El Shaddai? After the usual period for a pregnancy I'll return and Sarah shall have a son."

Color drained from Sarah's face as she rose and swayed on her feet to the tent door. In a shaky voice she said, "I didn't laugh."

The speaker turned and looked at her. "But you did laugh."

The men stood and prepared to leave. Abraham, as a good host, walked a ways with them.

Silence and heat gripped the three women. *Who is that man?* Hagar wondered. *Could Sarah really have a son?* Then a sudden and intolerable thought drove her to her feet. She stumbled and ran from

Sarah's tent to the security of her own. An old ache returned as she remembered 13 years before when El Shaddai had told her about Ishmael. Could He be sending Sarah a son? Why?

"Sarah is troubled," Inara said as she entered Hagar's tent. "She is so shaken that she doesn't want to talk"—the woman paused and stared at Hagar. "What's the matter?"

"If Sarah has a son," Hagar moaned, "would he take Ishmael's place as Abraham's heir?"

"Don't worry, Ishmael is the firstborn."

Hagar swiped at her tears. "Ishmael *must* be the father of kings on the thrones of kingdoms as great as Egypt," she vowed.

That night the heat lessened. Abraham's people listened as he related an incredible experience. "I entertained El Shaddai and two angels today," he announced. Murmurs of surprise spread through the gathering. Abraham held up his hands for silence. "El Shaddai again promised Sarah and me a son, and this time within a year."

Hagar noticed looks of disbelief pass cross the faces of those near her. *After all, they've heard this for 25 years,* she thought to herself. She glanced at Meret who winked at her.

"I walked a long way with them when they left," Abraham continued. "Suddenly El Shaddai said to me, 'Why should I hide from you what I'm about to do? Since you'll be a mighty nation and through you all nations will be blessed, I'll make it known to you. I'll tell you because you'll command your children and household after you to keep my way. I've come to destroy Sodom because its sins are very great.'

"This filled me with grief for Lot's family and the people of Sodom, so I reasoned with El Shaddai. 'Will you destroy the righteous with the wicked? Can you save the city if there are 50 righteous in it?'

"El Shaddai answered, 'If I find 50 righteous in Sodom I'll spare it for their sakes.'

"Knowing what Sodom is like, I asked what if there were five less, would He still destroy it? 'No, I'll save it for 45,' He replied.

"But I felt that I had to try again, and asked for him to leave the city alone if there were only 40. El Shaddai said that he would.

Getting even bolder, I said, 'Don't become angry with your servant. Will you save it for 30?'

"El Shaddai's welcome words were, 'I'll save it for 30.'

"Still feeling uneasy about Sodom's condition, I asked about the possibility for 20. El Shaddai assured me that He would not destroy it if there were at least 20.

"But something compelled me to try once more, so I pled, 'Let not El Shaddai be angry. I'll speak only once more. Will you save it for 10?'

"He said softly, 'I'll not destroy it for 10.' Then our divine guests started toward Sodom and I came back here. Praise our God. El Shaddai is a just God. The only true God. Let's get rest while it is cool. Tomorrow may be another hot day."

As everyone headed to their tents Hagar walked with a heart of lead. Constantly she told herself, *There's nothing to this son business. It will pass.*

The next morning she saw Abraham winding his way along the path he had taken with his guests the day before. An unknown fear gripped her for he walked as though life lay heavily upon him. Later she heard his choking voice say to Sarah, "I went to the spot where I stood with El Shaddai yesterday. While I looked down on Sodom and Gomorrah I saw them go up in smoke." Then she heard him weep.

Abimelech

When three days passed after the departure of the destruction of Sodom and no word came from Lot, Abraham mourned his loss. Hagar, and the camp, felt his restless spirit. A southeast wind picked up gritty ash from Sodom and dumped it on Mamre. Some in the camp wondered if they would also be destroyed.

That evening Abraham said that he could no longer bear to be near what had once been Lot's home. "The winter rains, four moons away, will revive the pastures in the south along the caravan routes to Egypt. We shall migrate to there."

After the inhabitants of Mamre shook down the olives and crushed them in the presses, the camp was ready for moving. With a sufficient supply of the first pressed oil and with ample food packed, Abraham's camp started south. They settled between Kadesh and Shur near a tiny oasis.

The shepherds located landowners willing to rent out their land as pasture but the rains would have to come soon if they were to have any grass. But since merchants considered winter and early spring the best time to travel through the desert, Abraham and Khuni expected that their caravans would prosper. Soon after their arrival Abraham spoke to Hagar after the evening sacrifice. "We are near Beer Lahai Roi where the angel spoke to you. Let's take Ishmael there tomorrow."

The next morning Abraham, Sarah, Ishmael, Hagar, Inara, and a number of servants made the short trip on fast camels.

"Here we are," Abraham announced, halting his camel in the small oasis. When they all dismounted from their kneeling animals, he continued, "I've long wanted to come to the place where El Shaddai named my son." He put his arm around Ishmael's shoulders and drew him close.

Hagar hastened to a spot near the well and, looking at Ishmael, said, "I stood in this holy spot when the angel told me to call you Ishmael (El Shaddai hears). He said your descendants would be too numerous to count."

Sarah said nothing as Abraham and Ishmael built a small altar of stones and offered a half-grown lamb one of the servants had brought with them. In a happy voice Abraham prayed, "El Shaddai, hear us from this hallowed spot where You named our son. You are gracious and kind to your servant for You have given me Ishmael, a fine son whom I love. And I look forward to another son by Sarah in harmony with the promise made before Sodom's destruction."

Her heart skipping a beat, Hagar she heard no more. Abraham's words dampened the joy of the trip. *What would a son by Sarah mean for Ishmael?* Her thoughts raced. *Is Sarah with child?*

Within a moon their stretch of southern wilderness became dry as the desert. The watercourses were long empty, and dust powdered everything. "We can't wait for the winter rains," Abraham said. "We must hasten north to the valley of Gerar. It is a land of pasture and grain fields."

Once the camp had settled in, Hagar eyed the rugs and other furnishings newly organized in her tent. Abraham had said they would stay at Gerar for a long time if Abimelech, the local ruler, was agreeable. She hastened to the supply tent where she directed the women storing food. A man's gruff voice rose above the clamor of those unloading the pack animals. Hagar lifted a tent flap not yet staked down and saw a tall man followed by three servants walk with long irregular strides toward Abraham and Eliezer. Slipping out of the tent, she stationed herself near some piles of supplies from which she could direct the women and still hear most of the men's conversation.

Sarah's work took her in and out of her tent nearby and all the servants in the area labored quietly, listening carefully to everything that went on.

"I'm Abimelech, king of Gerar," the tall man announced as

Abraham bowed to him. "Eliezer told me of your coming. You are many in number."

"We're around 1,000."

"And such vast herds. But our land can feed and water them and your people."

"This place indeed has ample pasture land. Our God, El Shaddai, has led us here."

"And you'll trade with us in Gerar?" Abimelech asked hopefully.

"With your permission."

"And your caravans will bring things to us?"

"Yes, from both the north and the south."

"Abraham, my friend, we must have an alliance between your people and mine. The Hittites are edging down from the north. If they invade this area, we may need each other."

"King of Gerar, your words are wise." Abraham bowed again. "When we know each other better we can work out the details."

"That will please me." He glanced toward Sarah's tent. "May I ask who that beautiful woman is over there?"

Abraham's answer was short—"She's my sister."

Abimelech looked back at Abraham. "Lucky you are. You'll hear from me again." He and his men turned to leave.

"Eliezer and I will accompany you to the edge of the camp," Abraham said, falling into step with him.

During the next few days they continued to unpack and store supplies. When everything was in order Hagar began to acquaint herself with her surroundings. In the late afternoons she and Inara began to explore the edge of the camp.

One day when they returned to camp they found Abraham and Sarah quite disturbed. As they approached Abraham commanded them to come to him. "Is there trouble?" Hagar asked out of curiosity.

"It's a disaster. Abimelech sent his emissaries to announce that 'the king has decided to make my beautiful sister his wife.' His servants will come for her and her maids in three days."

Hagar glanced at the angry Sarah who snapped, "I'm not going."

"Sarah, it will endanger the whole camp to refuse," he pleaded. "El Shaddai will again work it out."

"Why does he need another wife?" Inara asked. "Doesn't he already have enough beautiful women in his palace?"

"True, but he's intrigued with Sarah. He may think this will strengthen an alliance between us."

The husband and wife discussed the problem for some time. Something familiar about the situation nagged at the back of Hagar's thoughts. Abraham repeated the danger that the camp faced if Abimelech decided to take her by force. "I'll go, Abraham," she said at last. "I don't want anyone hurt. Will you have the camp pray for me and my maid?"

He nodded. "Tell me who you want to go with you."

She glanced at the two women. "Hagar and Inara. I'll choose some more later."

Instinctively Hagar knew that Sarah had picked her to keep her away from Abraham. But she asked anyway, "Why did you select me?"

Sarah searched her face. "Because you know how to be an attendant in a palace."

"Go get your things ready," Abraham told the two servants. "I'll tell the camp tonight to intercede with El Shaddai." He turned to Sarah. "Remember, El Shaddai promised you'd bear my son. He'll bring you back."

As Abimelech's servants escorted them into the ugly rambling palace, Hagar caught the smell of spices. A faint odor of cooking still hung in the air. In one room that they passed she stared at a table strewn with gnawed bones and pools of spilled wine.

The king had assigned a small cramped room to Sarah's servants but she had a larger one. Hagar had walked barefoot in her tent, unafraid of the little creatures of the wilderness. Now the spiders, lizards, and mice in the rambling palace freely ran over her feet. She found boots and shoved her feet into them.

Shortly before dark some palace servants brought a lamp, bread, and dried fruit. Hagar rose just as Inara slipped in, bringing her food. "What do you think of Abimelech's palace?"

"I'd rather live in a tent."

Before they ate they looked out a tiny window. In the street they saw the flare of torches. "Inara, this window's too small to slip through."

"You're going to try to escape?"

"I miss Ishmael and those at camp."

"I do too, but we had better see what happens here. Sarah may need us."

The first day they wandered aimlessly through each other's rooms, indulging in small talk. Sarah remained remote and solemn. When a palace servant brought them food, Hagar asked, "What can we do?"

The servant shrugged. "We have no instructions. Abimelech is sick. He'll see Princess Sarah when he's well." The second day went by like the first only it seemed longer.

When gifts of spices, cosmetics, and jewelry arrived for Sarah, she asked, "May a servant take me and my attendants for a walk through the city?" He soon returned with several more servants and told the women to follow them.

The longing in Sarah's voice was evident when she told Hagar and Inara, "Let's see if any of our people are trading in the city today."

The noise, filth, and smells in the market place disgusted the women. As Sarah looked around, she said, "We must help these people." In spite of herself Hagar felt a fleeting moment of admiration for her mistress.

The next day the palace servants sent them to an outside courtyard. Through the door at one end came a small neat woman followed by several attendants. Hagar guessed her to be in her forties though her face was not weathered nor did she have any hint of gray in the great coils of soot-black hair piled round and round on her head. Her eyes, black and lively, darted to Sarah and held her as they approached each other.

"You're Sarah. How fair you are. I'm Abimelech's chief wife, queen of Gerar."

"Abimelech is greatly honored to have you as a wife," Sarah greeted her. "You must be a help to him—and so young. I do not understand why he wants to marry me."

The woman became more reserved. "He believes marriage to

you will strengthen an alliance between your people and our people," she said carefully.

"But why is he eager for an alliance?"

"He believes that the Hittites will one day be in our land and wants to be prepared. All rulers make such covenants through marriage."

"Abraham and his people serve a special God, El Shaddai, who gives us protection," Sarah explained.

"We know of this God. He destroyed Sodom and the cities of the plain for their evil ways. Abimelech likes El Shaddai."

"But El Shaddai wants me to stay with my people," Sara protested.

"Abimelech may not agree. When he's well he will talk with you."

Two days dragged by with little contact with the rest of the palace. The late summer heat prostrated both humans and animals. During their walks with Sarah, Hagar and Inara still did not see anyone from their camp in the marketplace. Sarah's concern grew daily when no word came from Abraham.

"Inara," Hagar said, "I've found a way to climb to the roof. Let's walk there. It will soon be evening and cooler." Sarah went with them to the roof where they watched the sun slide toward the horizon, turning the hills and trees crimson and purple.

Hagar stared across the valley to the hill where the lights from the cooking fires began to appear in the growing darkness. Ishmael was there. Was he lonely without her? Suddenly anger replaced the longing. Careful not to look at her mistress, she said, "Sarah, if it weren't because of you, we'd be home over there tonight."

Hagar felt Inara's warning touch on her arm. Sarah did not reply. When Hagar saw the sorrow on Sarah's face, she felt a twinge of pity.

More and more people brought bedding to the surrounding rooftops to escape the heat inside. "Let's sleep here tonight," Inara suggested.

Just before sunrise Hagar jerked awake to the harsh anger of a man's voice. It came from a roof across the court. "Nevertheless," the man shouted, "do as I say. Have Abraham here immediately after dawn. I've suffered enough at his hands." Hagar's heart seemed to stop.

Her companions awoke and listened with her. They discussed what it could possibly mean until Sarah said, "Let's wait and see what happens. Remember, El Shaddai is in charge."

Later a fearful palace servant ushered Sarah and her attendants into Abimelech's reception chamber. Abraham and Eliezer, wearing puzzled expressions, stood at the opposite end of the room. When the women started to say something, Abraham immediately motioned them to silence.

Servants escorted Abimelech into the room. Hagar could see that he was ill. His clothing hung loosely upon him. "What have you done to us?" he demanded when he saw Abraham. His voice trembled as he continued, "How have I offended you? Why did you do this thing to us?"

Abraham bowed and with concern, said, "Your majesty, I'm but your servant. Why do you question us in this manner?"

Weak from his illness, Abimelech slumped into a chair. "Last night El Shaddai came to me in a dream. He said, 'Abimelech, you are about to die for you are planning to take another man's wife.' When I told him that you had said, 'She is my sister,' El Shaddai agreed that I was innocent. He explained that He had kept me from touching her by bringing sickness upon me and my household." Exhausted, Abimelech paused.

When he had regained some strength, he continued, "I remembered Sodom, so I asked El Shaddai if he would also destroy a righteous nation. El Shaddai said, 'Restore to the man his wife for he is a prophet. He shall pray for you and you will live.'"

Abraham stared at the king, then bowed. "O King Abimelech, as your servant I have told you a true thing. Sarah is my sister as well as my wife. I thought the fear of El Shaddai wasn't in this place and that I'd be slain to get my wife. Ever since God has led me to wander the land, I have asked Sarah to tell everyone that she is my brother. This is the second time it has caused trouble."

His voice stronger, Abimelech said, "I'll restore your wife. My servants will gather sheep and oxen, menservants and maidservants and give them to you. Behold my land is before you. Dwell where it pleases you." Then he ordered a servant to bring him a thousand pieces of silver.

Abimelech turned to Sarah. "I'm giving silver to your brother to right the wrong I have done to you and those with you."

Then Abraham prayed to El Shaddai who healed Abimelech and his household.

Isaac's Birth

At last Hagar awoke again in her own tent. Rising, she picked up her harp and walked to a spot that had already become a favorite. She sat on a small boulder behind a larger one that hid her from most of the camp. As she balanced the harp in her lap she watched the sun spread a soft pink glow over the land.

"I thought I'd find you here."

Startled, Hagar glanced over her shoulder at Inara. "I didn't see you coming."

"What were you doing?"

"Counting tents. I can see 321."

"There's a lot of them you can't see from here."

"I know. Abraham has hundreds of black tents, but when Ishmael is chief he'll have thousands." Hagar started to pluck her harp.

After they had sung several songs together Hagar laid aside her harp and crossed to another boulder. Resting her elbows on it, she cupped her chin in her hands and gazed northeast to where Sodom had once been.

"Look, Inara, the land of Sodom is so far away. We can hardly see it yet we know it's desolate and empty."

Closing her eyes, Hagar called up an image of the three visitors who had predicted the destruction of the cities of the plain.

Inara, as if sensing her thoughts, commented, "I often wonder about the strange visitors who warned Abraham of Sodom's fate."

Hagar opened her eyes. "It's the other part of the prediction that worries me."

"You mean the promise that Sarah will have a son within a year?"

"Yes. Do you think it can happen?"

With a sudden smile Inara said, "You imagine too much, Hagar."

"But Abraham says El Shaddai has made the promise twice recently that it will happen in a year. I'm afraid of what it might mean."

"Hagar, I've heard about that promise again and again for 24 years. Look how old Sarah is now. If Abraham wants another son he should think of you."

"You know he's refused many times to give me more children."

"Only because of Sarah's opposition."

Hagar picked up her harp. "Sarah seems rather happy lately. She doesn't talk much to me."

"It's been five and a half moons since the visitors came. If Sarah's pregnant she and Abraham aren't talking."

Each passing day Hagar felt uneasy. She asked herself again and again, "Do I really believe the promise the three visitors made?" Yet the fact of Sodom's destruction somehow made her think that Sarah might indeed have a child.

One evening as they were eating together, Ishmael told his mother, "Father told me Sarah might have a son who would be my brother."

"Did your father say that Sarah was going to have a son or she *might* have one?"

"He said 'might' but he sounded as if he believed that she would. He was happy about it."

"Ishmael, make your father feel that he needs you—that—that he can't get along without you. Remember that you're his firstborn and his heir no matter what happens."

"I do. And he tells me what kind of leader I should be when he turns everything over to me."

Hagar sat back on her heels and her expression became serious. "Ishmael, remember to report to me everything you hear about Sarah."

"I don't hear much but I'll remember."

Day after day Hagar eyed Sarah, looking for any sign of pregnancy. After seven moons she thought she saw a change in Sarah's shape, but even more evident was her glow and animation as she worked and talked to the women.

One night at the fire Hagar whispered, "Inara, does Sarah look pregnant to you?"

Inara placed her mouth close to Hagar's ear. "This morning I thought she might be. Don't worry, El Shaddai promised that Ishmael would found a great nation."

A mirthless laugh escaped Hagar's lips. "I'm afraid," she whispered loudly, "that Sarah will make sure that her son replaces Ishmael as heir."

As the days sped by Hagar still heard nothing from Sarah herself about expecting a child. She did overhear one of the servants comment to another, "Sarah is getting heavy and slow in her old age."

As the year drew to a close, Hagar's uneasiness intensified. Eleven moons had passed since the visit of the three supernatural visitors. One day she noticed that Sarah had difficulty bending over. Without thinking, Hagar asked, "Sarah are you . . ." She swallowed. The unspoken words pierced her heart like spears. Sarah silently stared at her for some moments, then turned back to her work.

Early one afternoon Hagar saw Sarah go into the midwife's tent and remain there. Searching for work to keep her busy in front of her tent, she brought out the brazier and placed it so she could see the birthing tent. *I'll roast these garbanzos,* she told herself, *while I watch for Sarah.* She saw Abraham pace back and forth in front of his tent. After a time he sat down, wrapped his arms around his legs, and rested his head upon his knees.

From time to time she thought she heard Sarah moan. Suddenly the angry wail of a newborn caused him to dash into the tent—and Hagar knew Sarah was no longer childless. Soon the blare of the shofar announced the birth to the whole camp.

All of Hagar's nagging little worries congealed into one great fear and a sense of desolation overwhelmed her. Stumbling into her tent, she threw herself on her bed. Her heart pounded in her head.

That night only a thin sickle of a moon hung in the sky. Hagar could not sleep. Memories raced through her thoughts—the years in the Egyptian household of the women, her decision to follow Sarah and her God El Shaddai, the birth of Ishmael. Finally came grief and anguished sobs.

In the days that followed Hagar noticed that her bitterness began to infect her son but she didn't care. The joy and celebration that filled the tents of Abraham and Sarah only intensified the jealousy in Hagar and Ishmael.

All his life he had expected to inherit Abraham's wealth and the promised blessing. Now Isaac's birth had suddenly thrust him aside. In their disappointment Hagar and Ishmael now hated Sarah's child.

The Weaning

Hagar heard a rumble like thunder mixed with the howls of a wild wind. Ma'at vanished and the world plunged back into chaos as she tumbled into darkness and despair. Terror seized her like a wild animal and shook her until she thought she would be torn apart. Then she jolted awake and realized that it was only a dream.

Wind flapped the tent walls back and forth with a monotonous snap. In the distance the flutes of shepherds mingled with the brays of donkeys and the sounds of human voices. Hagar remembered that preparations were in progress for the feast celebrating Isaac's weaning. Inara brought food and together they breakfasted on bread, cheese, dried figs, and warm milk. "Before I do anything else I want to find out what's going on in camp," Hagar told her.

They walked to the sun-warmed east side of the tent where Inara began to grind barley. "I will finish the flour before noon," she said.

"Good. Then go to Eliezer. Ask him to send a donkey boy with enough barley, wheat, melon seeds, lentils, chickpeas, and beans to last a week. Also roast plenty of chickpeas."

"I will," Inara promised.

Hagar looked far out over the Beersheba Basin. The gradual slope of the elongated valley rose eastward to Beersheba and the plain of Arad. To the north the curved lines of the mountains led her gaze to the east. The labyrinth of peaks and gullies plunged down into the Dead Sea Valley where Sodom had once been. They painfully reminded her of the three visitors and the promise of Isaac. To the south the mountains dissolved into broken hill country and desert.

The heavy rains of the past winter had replenished the water

174

springs. The land was green with grass and barley and wheat. During the upcoming dry season everything would turn brown and dusty. But now crimson flowers dotted the rocky landscape. Hagar reached for the long feathery branches of the gnarled tamarisk beside her tent. In a few days spikes of pink blossoms would cover the tree. The land of the Sand-dwellers was a beautiful one, but the pain in her heart dimmed its allure.

In the distance a caravan of donkeys wound its way toward them. Hagar knew that it brought raisins, date and fig cakes, nuts, oil, sesame seed, and other things for Isaac's feast. The thought tore at her heart as she went in search of Sarah.

Hagar found Sarah directing some of the servants as they placed water jars in the eight-pole tent that would house guests. She turned to Hagar. "This afternoon have someone bring more rugs, skins, cushions, and blankets here," she said. "Sprinkle cypress oil on the floor, then put down mats and rugs. Melchizedek and his wife will stay in these rooms."

Finally everything was ready and Abraham's people waited for their guests. The women had prepared bountiful supplies of food. Many had new clothes for the occasion. Shepherds who wished to attend the celebration brought their flocks and herds to nearby pastures in shifts.

Hagar expected the guests at Isaac's feast to regard Ishmael as Abraham's heir. She was sure they would recognize that he had his father's wisdom and leadership skills.

"After we eat let's go to Meret's tent," she suggested to Inara. "From there it will be easier to watch people arrive."

The first guests arrived by midmorning. They were the royal brothers, Mamre, Aner, and Eschol, men with dark hair and eyes and big grins. Then came those from more distant villages. Abraham detailed servants to help the visitors locate their tents as close as possible but still outside his camp circle. The servants carried jars of water to the guests and washed the dust of travel from their feet. Hagar, with Inara, walked around camp to see all who had come. It especially excited Hagar when those who could spoke to her in Egyptian.

Abimelech and others from Gerar arrived in the afternoon.

Melchizedek's family and servants appeared later. As the guests milled about the crowded camp their voices and laughter ebbed and flowed. Now and then Hagar caught words spoken in more distant languages. As the day declined into evening shadows mothers crooned over sleeping babies and men stretched weary limbs.

The Mocking

Hagar slipped into her tent to rebraid her hair and put on a headband. Just as she finished a snatch of overheard conversation seized her attention. "Do you think Isaac is Sarah's child?" one woman said to another. "She's in her nineties, you know."

"I wonder if a slave bore Isaac," the other replied.

Curious, Hagar raised the tent flap. Noticing her, a woman that Hagar recognized as from Gerar asked, "May I come in?"

"Please do," Hagar said.

Once inside the woman said, "Hagar, will you tell me something?"

"Of course, if I can."

"Did Sarah give birth to Isaac?"

At first the question shocked Hagar, but then an idea popped into her mind. What if people had doubts about the legitimacy of Isaac's birth? Could such questions help ensure Ishmael's rightful place? A plan began to sprout in her heart.

"Why do you ask?" she hedged.

"I must know if a miracle occurred. I hope so, but some say Isaac must have a slave mother."

"I bore Ishmael but did not give him away," Hagar said on impulse. "He is Abraham's firstborn, Isaac is his second." Hagar saw the disappointment on her face and dared say no more.

After a moment the woman said, "I see," and left.

Shortly afterward Hagar left the tent and headed for the archery field where she knew Ishmael would be practicing. As she passed little clusters of women talking among themselves the women would often pause to glance her way. A proverb she had once heard came to mind: "The whispers of gossips are like savory morsels."

Inara joined her. "What sends you to the archery field? Is it Ishmael you want to watch?"

"In all the years you've served me I've never learned to hide things from you. You know I'm upset."

"I guessed as much."

"Inara, have you heard any gossip in camp about Isaac?"

"No, should I have?"

"If you do, tell me. What do you think of Ishmael? Be honest."

"Hagar, I wish I had a son like him. He's a rich man's son who must share his father's attention with Isaac."

"All the attention that Abraham and everyone else in camp give Isaac offers him an unfair advantage. To counteract it I try to make sure that Ishmael is with his father as much as possible."

"You should do less for him and let Abraham do more."

Hagar sighed. "Children are to parents like a quiver of arrows, but I've only one son to send forth."

"Your son is long on energy and short on common sense. Let his father handle his future."

"Inara!" Hagar closed her eyes and frowned. "You don't understand. All the shepherds desire his help. Does that show he's short on common sense?"

"I'm just being honest."

Hagar changed the subject. "It looks as if everyone has come to see the archery competition. I see they have the targets ready." She and Inara found a shady spot to sit.

Other women found places beside them. "Hagar, Ishmael is so handsome," one woman commented. "Do you think Isaac will grow to be as handsome?"

"They have the same father," Hagar answered after a hesitation.

"But different mothers," several said at the same time.

"Hagar, we know Sarah is too old to bear children," one woman interjected. "Who is the slave who bore Isaac for her?"

A silence followed as Hagar glanced down, embarrassed.

"Tutu, don't question Hagar," someone said. "She is loyal to Sarah."

Nods passed between the women. Hagar heard the names of

Isaac or Ishmael mentioned. She saw raised brows as the group seemed to be coming to the same conclusion.

"What are they saying?" Inara whispered.

"We'll find out later. Look, they're ready to start."

The contestants had piled up grass into a series of staggered targets The men would shoot at them from a distance of 75 to 200 cubits.

Each archer had several bows and a leather quiver full of various kinds of arrows. Ishmael's favorite bow was a long one strengthened with leather plaiting and a strong linen cord. Most of his arrow points he had fashioned from flint, ivory, or bone, but he did have a few prized bronze points that Abraham had given him. The bow was his chief weapon for hunting. The boy had spent much time with the herdsmen practicing, and the shepherds proudly claimed that no one could shoot arrows straighter than he did.

Hagar saw Eliezer approaching. When he reached the field he organized the judges then lined up the contestants in the order they would compete. In his Aramaic accent he called each archer to let his arrows fly fast and far. Ishmael aimed at the farthest target. Again and again he hit its center and cheers rose from the observers.

Isaac wandered from his nursemaid onto the archery field, intent to be with his brother. "Get back!" Ishmael shouted at the child.

But Isaac didn't move. "Isaac want shoot," he pleaded.

"No, Isaac." Ishmael picked him up, set him down at the edge of the field, and started back to his position. The child raced after Ishmael, crying loudly and grabbing him around the leg. "Shoot. Isaac want shoot," he begged.

Everyone grew quiet, watching the scene. "You can't even hold a bow by yourself," Ishmael yelled at the boy. "You're spoiled and— and you're not Abraham's firstborn son." Then he shoved Isaac to the edge of the field where the nursemaid met them and took the crying boy back to camp.

Those who had seen the incident began to discuss it among themselves. From the way they shook their heads Hagar gathered that many disapproved of what he had done. *He's too rough with Isaac,* she thought.

At last the archery contest came to an end. The judges announced the winners in the different rounds and called Ishmael's name frequently. Then the young men fell to discussing the merits of their particular bows and arrows. The rest clustered in groups to talk or headed back to their tents. Aromas of roasting lamb and other food sharpened appetites for the feast to be held later that day.

As Hagar and Inara walked toward their tents Khuni and Meret joined them. "Hagar, have you or Inara heard the gossip circulating among the guests?" he questioned.

"What talk?" Hagar asked cautiously.

"That Isaac is the son of a slave. The idea is widespread among the guests, men as well as women. The men question the legal status of Abraham's two sons. Some have commented that you show your loyalty to Sarah because you refuse to tell who Isaac's real mother is." Khuni's eyes searched hers.

"Several have asked me who Isaac's real mother is," she said uncomfortably, "but I have told them nothing. They're just jumping to conclusions."

Khuni stared at her in amazement. "Why didn't you tell them Isaac is Sarah's own child, a child of promise? That would stop the whispers. Do you realize the implications of these rumors?"

His eyes had a way of looking into her heart. Choking down anger, she forced a smile. "Are you criticizing me? You speak as though you're my master."

Anger flashed across his face. "If I were your master this wouldn't happen." He was about to say more, but then another emotion suddenly overcame him. His body shook with laughter and Hagar found herself growing even angrier. Eventually he gained control of himself. "Hagar, was this your way to make sure Ishmael remained Abraham's heir?"

"You don't always have to tell the whole truth," she spat out with sarcasm.

"Hagar, are you trying to thwart El Shaddai? It won't work." Khuni was a practical and decisive man. "I must ask Eliezer to report these rumors to Abraham." Then he turned to meet the steward as he left the archer's field and walked with him toward camp. Nearby Inara talked to Meret and her children. Hagar, left alone, brushed away tears then pushed through the crowd and swept into her tent. Once inside her tears came like a cloudburst rushing down a wadi.

Inara opened the tent flap, paused, then said gently, "You'd look better if you stopped crying and sat up straight." She poured water into a basin and handed it to Hagar who washed her face, neck, feet, and hands. Then Inara smoothed her hair just as the ram's horn sounded the summons to the feast.

Servants had spread mats end-to-end near the eight-pole tent. The feast menu included roast lamb, barley stew, wheat and parsley salad, beans, lentils, chickpeas, and pine nuts. For the first time Abraham took Isaac to eat with the men. There he sat on Abraham's right as the honored one while Ishmael sat on his left. The feast was in honor of Isaac, and Hagar had misgivings about what it might represent for the future.

After the women and children took their places, Abraham signaled for silence and thanked El Shaddai for their guests, his sons, and the abundant food. When the prayer ended they all broke bread into pieces to scoop food. Some food they rolled into balls and with their thumbs flipped it into their mouths. At times someone would burst into song and others joined in. There were songs from Ur, Damascus, and Egypt. Last they chose to adapt a Sumerian song to honor Abraham.

"His heart is like a shrine,
His words are like prayers,
His utterances supplications,
His feasts flow with fat and milk,
They are rich with abundance.
His storehouses bring happiness and rejoicing.
Abraham's house, because of El Shaddai,
Is a mountain of plenty.
His sons will rise to honor him."

The reference to the sons made Hagar uncomfortable, and she glanced toward Abraham and Sarah to see what kind of mood they were in. *They don't seem upset,* she thought to herself. *Perhaps they haven't learned about the rumors. Maybe everything will be all right.*

After they had eaten Abraham had the servants distribute gifts to each guest to show his appreciation for their presence. Then Sarah did the same for the women. While the guests admired their gifts the servants brought water to wash food from their right hands and towels to dry them. As the feast ended Eliezer announced, "The evening sacrifice will be early tonight."

While Hagar and Inara walked toward their tents two women ahead stopped to wait for them. The older one approached Hagar. "Tell us about Isaac."

"What about him?"

"Abraham and Sarah are old! They must have picked up a foundling somewhere. Now they pretend he's their own son and to make it appear credible they arrange a feast in his honor."

Amazed, Hagar studied the women while her heart stood paralyzed. *The rumors grow and take on new dimensions,* she thought.

"Hagar, you're a wife of Abraham," the first woman continued. "What do you know about this child? Which bondmaid is his real mother? From where did he come?"

"I don't wish to talk about Isaac," Hagar replied.

"Many would like to know the facts," the woman insisted, annoyance in her voice.

"It is not my place to say anything," she stammered. She glanced toward Inara. "We must leave now."

"Why didn't you tell them Isaac is a miracle born to Sarah?" Inara demanded when they reached the tent.

"I don't know—I mean I want Ishmael's rights as firstborn."

"Abraham is always fair."

"Yes, but something about Isaac makes me uneasy."

"What are you afraid of? Ishmael has a royal heritage from you as well as his father. Has he never received anything less than complete respect?"

Hagar squeezed her eyes shut, trying to stop the flow of tears. "Inara, I want to do everything I can to protect his right as Abraham's heir."

Inara sighed. "I know that Isaac's birth makes you uneasy, but I've told you repeatedly that things will work out just as El Shaddai promised you!"

The Promise Fulfilled

At the sound of the ram's horn Hagar and Inara hurried to the center of the camp. "Look." Inara pointed. "A new altar. Why?"

"Because of Isaac," Hagar surmised.

"How could that be?"

Hagar shrugged.

Sarah and Isaac sat close to where Abraham stood. After raising his arms for silence, he then reached for Isaac, lifted him, and held him in his arms. "On our last night together at this feast," he began in a firm, clear voice, "I want to share a promise made almost 30 years ago. You know El Shaddai promised a son by Sarah. When I was 100 and Sarah was 90 years the promised son was born. By this feast I share my joy of Isaac's birth with you."

Hagar realized that she was holding her breath as Abraham continued. "Sarah and I are full of praise for El Shaddai's fulfillment of His promise. I've asked Sarah to nurse Isaac one last time before the celebration is over." Hagar heard a gasp behind her and saw people look at each other in bewilderment. "That way you'll see that he's her child." Then he led Isaac to his wife. Her face glowed as she nursed the hungry child. The crowd caught its breath as they viewed the scene.

The whimper of another child broke the silence and the woman named Tutu called out, "My son is hungry. May Sarah nurse him?"

"Bring him here," Abraham replied calmly.

Tutu brought her small son and stayed by Sarah as he hungrily nursed. When he grew sleepy Tutu took him from Sarah's breast and rocked him in her arms.

Abraham's guests now knew without doubt that Sarah was Isaac's mother.

Hagar sensed people glancing at her. She struggled to appear at ease and unconcerned, but fear churned in the pit of her stomach. *Abraham has implicated no one,* she tried to reassure herself. With a simple demonstration he solved the doubt lingering over Isaac's birth. All hope fled as she realized that it was becoming clear that Isaac, not Ishmael, would be heir. She wanted to flee to the security of her tent but everyone would notice if she left now.

Abraham went to the stone altar. Then he picked up the nearby lamb and soothed away its bewildered bleating. A solemn silence fell on everyone. The patriarch continued to stroke the creature's neck as he spoke in a low deep voice. "Because this ceremony will be a vital part of the life of Isaac's descendants, we want all of you to share this moment with us as we offer the evening sacrifice to El Shaddai."

Now Abraham's voice held an ache of sadness. "I'll pray to El Shaddai to accept this sacrifice." It was as though he spoke face-to-face with his invisible God. "El Shaddai, creator of the universe, we thank You for Your continued blessings. Accept our offering of this lamb as we praise You for creating us and giving us sons through whom we may pass on life. We thank You for friends who are guests around our fire. They have come to celebrate with us Your fulfillment of Your promise of my son, Isaac. Give them a rich blessing. You have brought us to a good land of wheat and barley, vines and figs, and olives and wild honey. It sustains flocks and herds. May it receive Your blessing and may we live long in this place. So be it."

Abraham set the lamb down, raised a knife, and in an instant it lay bleeding beside the altar. Another kind of pain seared through Hagar.

Banished

Hagar ignored the muted voices of those on their way to the evening sacrifice. Pulling a mat from the stack in her tent, she threw it to the floor then sank upon it. Ever since Isaac's feast she had not attended either the morning or evening sacrifices. Neither had she spoken to Abraham or Sarah. She had hoped that the guests at the celebration would recognize Ishmael as the rightful heir. But it had not materialized. Instead, Abraham's successful demonstration that Sarah was indeed the child's mother had caused everyone to regard Isaac with awe. At the same time many in the camp had begun to resent Ishmael's attitude toward Isaac. Ever since the weaning Hagar had been unable to shake off a premonition of disaster.

As the gray of night crept out of the east, she saw Abraham walk along the path in front of the tents. He looked weary. Then her heart leaped as he turned toward her tent.

Since Ishmael's birth she had gone to Abraham for supplies, favors, or to voice complaints. But he had never visited her. Hope swelled inside her heart. *Maybe he comes to say he loves Ishmael and my son is still his heir.* But she knew it was a foolish thought.

For a moment he stood wordless at the edge of the tent. Rising to her feet, she reached for a mat and placed it near him. "You honor me with your presence," she said hesitantly. For a long moment they studied each other. The look in his eyes increased her apprehension. Nevertheless, she broke the silence, hoping her voice didn't betray her feelings.

"Abraham, rest a while." In spite of herself her voice trembled. At first he didn't reply.

185

As an ominous silence fell between them she felt as if he was preparing himself for some gigantic effort. She waited, troubled by the unfamiliar expression on his face, but it still surprised her when he asked, "Why don't you get along with Sarah?"

She could not answer. Unbidden memories stilled her words. A sharp pain cut into her numb heart. Again she probed his eyes but found in them only unhappiness. He was silent a long time.

"Hagar, you and Sarah don't get along," he said finally. "And Ishmael resents Isaac. I cannot let it tear the camp apart. I—I must ask you and Ishmael to dwell somewhere else." He paused to let his words sink in. She felt a sense of unreality.

Then the shock, delayed at first, hit her with an anger born of fear. "This sounds like Sarah!" she lashed back. "You are condemning us to death unless we can find another household to accept us! What you're doing is contrary to all the rules of society. We won't leave!"

Abraham stared at her, clearly struggling to find words. "Hagar, I've talked to El Shaddai. He promises to make of our son a great nation." He swallowed hard. Despite her own anger she still sensed the grief he was fighting back. "El Shaddai can do that even away from here."

Numbly she asked, "But where will we go?"

He glanced away, but not before she saw the tears glisten in his eyes. "Another shepherd's camp, perhaps."

Again anger exploded in her. "No! We'll go to Egypt."

"Visit Egypt if you will, but return here. You know that Sen Wosret has died. The land of Ishmael's birth will call him back. He will not be happy in the rigid society of your homeland. There is pasture in Paran. Make your home there." Again he lapsed into silence.

"When must we leave?" she asked wearily.

"Tomorrow morning will be best."

"Tomorrow? But we must pack! You are unfair to the son you once loved!"

He winced at her words. "You know that I still love our son. But it is best for everyone that you leave as soon as possible. Hagar, travel light for now. I will see to it that you will get your tents and goods later."

"But Ishmael is with the shepherds in the hills."

"I've sent for him and will talk with him. Ishmael's a man now and can understand. He'll sleep in his tent tonight."

The finality in his voice overwhelmed her. "It's not fair," she shouted as she sprang to her feet. "Sarah's not fair! You're not fair! Ishmael was supposed to be the heir. That's why he was born. Now Sarah says he stands in Isaac's way. If you claim everyone is equal before El Shaddai, why does He prefer Isaac?" She clenched her fists. "I . . . I . . . hate you!"

Sadly Abraham rose and with heavy steps returned by the way he had come. Hagar collapsed on her mat.

The finality of what had happened left her totally numb. She knew that she could not alter his decision. He could be as powerful and unyielding in his tribe as her father had been as pharaoh in Egypt. And Sarah would make sure that her husband did not change his mind. The horror of her situation washed over Hagar and left her nauseated, and she began to rock back and forth like a little child. Unable to even cry, she wailed like a tiny injured animal. Outside her tent the camp drifted into sleep.

"Hagar?"

Somehow the word—tinged with its own sorrow—managed to penetrate her grief. Slowly she staggered outside the tent. "Abraham?" She could she his outline in the darkness.

"Hagar, this heartache is my fault. I've come to ask you to forgive me." Once again her speech fled.

"I've wronged you. Sarah and I did wrong to ask you to bear us a child. We did not trust El Shaddai. In our human wisdom we tried to help Him fulfill His promise of a son. But our way was not El Shaddai's."

His plea for forgiveness threw her off balance by its very unexpectedness. Yet her reply was sharp but steady as she asked, "So? Do you disown Ishmael as your firstborn, your heir? Does his presence offend you?" Suddenly she realized that Abraham did not love her and never had. She had only been a means to an end. But at that moment the knowledge did not matter.

"Hagar, Ishmael was a mistake, but he's my son and I love him with all my heart. El Shaddai loves him too. He works with our

187

human mistakes. Ishmael will be the father of kings. Remember, I was 86 when he was born but you were so young. You deserved a husband all your own. Out of your loyalty to us you honored our request. Our plan brought you only untold sorrow, for you refused to give up your son. We can't always make life work the way we want it. Since we can't go back and do things over, I've asked El Shaddai's forgiveness. Hagar," he asked softly, "will you also forgive me?"

Slowly, as she stared at Abraham, her mind began to work again. In his plea for forgiveness she saw a new side to his character. An overwhelming awe akin to love surged through her heart as she saw how dignity and meekness blended together in the father of Ishmael. Abraham, the powerful tribal chieftain, could also feel humility and vulnerability. And it forced herself to face reality when to do so was only unbearable agony. Trembling, she reached to a nearby tree to steady herself.

As her mind raced through the years since Ishmael's birth she realized that she also had made wrong decisions, that she had used Abraham and Sarah just as much as they had used her. Only then did she break the silence, speaking slowly in tense, subdued tones.

"I must ask your forgiveness too. Because your heart was not filled with me, I wrongly demanded unfair things from you. Jealous of Sarah, I schemed to steal your affection from her. After all, I was the childbearing wife and wanted first place in your heart. In Egypt I had been only the daughter of a minor wife in my father's household. Ishmael was the only person whom I have been close to. I wanted his love for I had to be the center of somebody's life. Now I see my scheming has only ruined my life, his, Sarah's, and yours. If only I could live those years again."

With these words her anger ebbed, to be replaced by an overwhelming sense of desolation. Yet Abraham's request for forgiveness did bring a measure of comfort and strength. He waited for her to continue.

"Yes, Abraham, I—I do forgive you. But I too need forgiveness," she whispered.

"Hagar, you are forgiven. I'll meet you and Ishmael at dawn on the road to Beersheba."

"Where?"

"At the place where ledges of rock jut through the earth like bones through the skins of sheep long dead in the desert. I'll bring food and water. Take from your tent only necessities. Tomorrow will find you in Beersheba before night. I will send your tents, your household goods, your servants—and silver and gold." Then he vanished into the night.

Now at last her tears could come. Hagar dropped her head into her hands and wept. As the tears began to cease other memories flooded her heart. She remembered the care that Sarah and Abraham had lavished upon her. They had treated her like a daughter. But her ambition for Ishmael had turned her against them, especially Sarah. Once she had admired them so much that she chose to leave Egypt and worship their God. *Abraham is wise and understanding. Both have shown me much compassion and kindness. My campaign to assure Ishmael's birthright kept me from realizing how much I care for them. I've been a fool, and it has cost me the love of the two greatest people on earth.*

Hagar sat motionless for a long time. Then she glanced up at the night sky and saw Orion driving the fleeing Pleiades across the heavens. Returning to her tent she fell into a dreamless and exhausted sleep.

The Wilderness of Beersheba

When, after a few fleeting hours of sleep, Hagar hurried through the early-morning mist and arrived at the rocky outcropping along the road to Beersheba, Ishmael was already there. Tall and strong, he waited with his bow and quiver of arrows, throw stick, sling, bag of stones, and flute resting at his feet. His face clearly revealed his ancestry, but this morning he did not hold his head as a young prince. Except for his hands moving restlessly at his side, he stood like an image of stone. His hawklike eyes searched her face. In return her eyes studied his. In them she found no welcome, only resentment. She shivered and a hope died.

"You should have given me to Sarah," he accused, then stopped and watched her guardedly.

"Ishmael, your father loves you still," she said as she approached him, determined not to show her own grief. "I love you. You are the center of my life. I beg you to understand why I couldn't give you up, bone of my bone, and flesh of my flesh. I'm sorry. Will you forgive me?"

But he turned his eyes away and pain pierced her heart. She waited, watching the pulse beat in his neck. After a time his eyes, stabbing questions, came back to hers. With a struggle, he kept his features composed. His mouth opened but words refused to come. Then he choked out, "Mother, last night father asked me to forgive him."

Just then Abraham appeared out of the mist, the promised bag of bread and a waterskin over his shoulder. His face was a mask of grief as he turned to Ishmael. "My son, I wish this parting were not necessary. I love you. May you grow toward El Shaddai straight as the reed to the sun."

For a brief moment Hagar felt a sense of family as she stood there with father and son. "Abraham, will you visit Ishmael?" It was a desperate plea, one more effort to delay the parting. "Your son greatly admires you. Ishmael has always wanted to be like you."

"Yes," he said slowly, "when Ishmael has established himself. For now, send messages by caravan. Let me know of any need." He placed the water and food on her back. "Here are sufficient shekels of silver. Go to Beersheba, wait there until your possessions arrive, then head south into Paran. This goatskin of water will last until you reach the first well."

Turning again to his son, he put his arm around the young man's shoulders. On impulse Ishmael, his grief strained to the limit, clung to Abraham. "I love you father. I don't want to leave." His voice trembled and both men wept.

Finally Abraham disengaged himself from Ishmael's embrace. "Hagar, I'll pray for you each day." He looked at his son. "Ishmael, take care of your mother." With a sigh he turned back the way he had come.

Already the rays of the rising sun had cleared away the morning mist and promised a hot day. Mother and son watched Abraham until he vanished in the distance. Then with slow steps they took the road east to Beersheba. Soon the blazing sun seared their skin and baked the ground. They faced into the hot east wind, which dried their skin and intensified their thirst.

When they paused to rest, Ishmael turned to her and said angrily, "Mother, I'm denied my proper place for the sake of another. People call me wild and headstrong. So be it! I shall live up to the charge." His face wore a grim smile.

A prophecy she didn't like flashed from a corner of her heart. Even before his birth El Shaddai had said that Ishmael would be a wild man.

"Wait, can it not be said that 'Ishmael is like Abraham, honored by his father'? It is best for a son to accept his father's words," she cautioned. "Don't withdraw your heart from him."

He paused a moment, then said, "I'm devoted to father. I have heeded his teaching. But I can't understand why he would send us away."

"Ishmael, my people have a proverb that declares, 'Seeing, hearing, breathing all report to the heart to make understanding come forth.' Be patient."

As the sun climbed higher and the wind quickened their dehydration the goatskin grew lighter and lighter until it was empty. "This wind is like that from the bellows of a metal smith's fire," Ishmael complained. "It makes the sun even hotter."

"Yes," she agreed. "The heat is bad."

"Where is the well?" he moaned later. "My tongue is like dry wool, my throat like sand, and my head aches."

Hagar knew that the bodies of the young lose moisture faster than older ones. A sleepless night had further sapped Ishmael's energy. She watched him dig wax from his ears and rub it over his cracked lips, a trick he had learned from the shepherds. Her own lips began to dry and crack. By now she was worried. Because the sun was high the lack of shadows flattened out the landscape. Even from a short distance it was easy to overlook familiar landmarks. Panic began to cloud her reason. Had they wandered from the road? She couldn't be sure. Nothing was familiar. They were lost somewhere south of Beersheba and had already missed several wells.

The heat began to make Ishmael delirious. Finally he threw himself onto the hot ground. "I can't go on," he moaned.

"Ishmael, we must. Come." She tugged at his limp body.

"No. Go," he whispered.

Panic-stricken, she pulled him into the scant shade of a tamarisk bush. She knew only a slender thread held him to life. Her heart turned to stone. It was too much. She couldn't bear to watch Ishmael die so she walked away as far from the tamarisk as a bowshot. *When he's dead, I'll return to die beside him.*

In her anguish she shouted to the silent desert, "Why did Abraham send us away alone? Why are people unjust? Why does El Shaddai let Ishmael die? Why? Why?" But her screaming only melted away in the hot wind.

The heat began to make her hallucinate. Images of the eternal city of the dead in Egypt floated before her like gnats in the summer sun. Silent pyramids reached into the blue sky beside the Nile. Such memories only deepened her grief. No way could they, like Sinuhe, be buried in the eternal home of the dead. Oh, how much she wanted a pillar of stone or a memory in the heart of her people. But here they'd die without even a sheepskin to cover them in the land of the Sand-dwellers. Their end was to be death in the wild desert. Vultures patiently sailed overhead. One flew so close that she could see it swivel its naked yellow head from side to side to bring each eye in turn to focus on them

"Go away," Hagar screamed at them. "You wish to make us as though we never were! Then the sun will burn our bones to powder for the wind to blow away. The gods will forget us. Our names will come to an end—and we perish forever!" The carrion bird circled and then drifted away.

"No, it's not fair!" she cried to the deaf wilderness. Suddenly her thoughts became clearer. "El Shaddai, you saved me once before," she said, her voice hoarse from lack of water. "Help us now. Provide us water or we perish. It would be unjust for You to let Ishmael's life vanish without a trace after You promised to make him a father of many kings. My cry will fill the whole earth for generations to come." Sobs wracked her body.

"Hagar, why do you weep?"

Stunned, she looked around but saw no one.

"El Shaddai has heard your son's cries. Don't be afraid. Take him by the hand. I'll make him a great nation as I promised you."

She knew she'd heard the same voice before Ishmael's birth. El Shaddai had spoken from heaven! He saw! He heard! He cared!

Hagar rushed to her dying son. "Ishmael, Ishmael! El Shaddai has heard your cries!" She pulled him to his feet. "Come. El Shaddai bids us go on."

Not far away she spotted the rock wall protecting a well. After helping Ishmael sit, she removed a few of the rocks and saw the shimmer of light on water. Quickly she filled their skin bottle. First she gave him a few careful sips. Next she took a few swallows herself. Then, after a bit, they each drank deeply.

Hagar watched Ishmael gather strength. "El Shaddai saw our trouble," he whispered. "Father must have asked Him to care for us."

She nodded. "Before you were born, the angel of El Shaddai said, 'You will bear a son. Give him the name Ishmael, which means El Shaddai hears.' Then the angel added, 'I will increase your descendants so they will be too numerous to count.' Now El Shaddai has once again promised, 'I will make of Ishmael a great nation. Kings shall come from him.'" Her hand dropped lightly upon his forehead and her fingers caught in his hair and lingered there.

"I thank El Shaddai. You're a good mother. I love you and I'll care for you."

Later, after they had rested and filled their waterskin, mother and son stood together for a moment. To the west the sun set over their former home, the land they had both loved. Hagar thought how she would miss Khuni and Meret, Eliezer, Abraham, and even Sarah and Isaac.

Their life in Abraham's camp had come to an end. That fact would hurt today and would hurt tomorrow and all the tomorrows of their lives. But El Shaddai would fill their lives with other things.

"We are like Pharaoh my father," she said. "Once in battle he snatched victory from defeat. We are heirs of courage and perseverance. And both you and I have learned much from your father Abraham and his God. With El Shaddai's help we will persevere." Together they started toward Paran, their future homeland.

Epilogue

While they lived in Paran, Hagar found an Egyptian wife for Ishmael. Possibly to be close to Ishmael, a son he truly loved, Abraham remained in the land of Abimelech a long time. Legends—perhaps faded memories filtered through the centuries—tell of visits that he made to Ishmael. It seems that after Sarah died Ishmael, his family, servants, and flocks sojourned for a time in his father's camp.

When Ishmael was 89 and Isaac 75 they together buried Abraham with Sarah in the cave of Machpelah near Mamre.

The Arabs today claim Abraham as their father. They are largely descendants through Ishmael, Abraham's six sons by Ketura (Zimram, Jokshan, Medan, Midian, Ishbak, Shua), and Abraham's grandson Esau. No doubt Lot's descendants and other Canaanites also melted into the present day Arab nations.

The Hagarites, a nomadic people south of Beersheba, may have been Hagar's descendants. During David's time some lived throughout Transjordan. A Hagarite cared for David's flocks.

Bibliography

Aldred, Cyril. *The Egyptians: Ancient Peoples and Places.* New York: Frederick A. Praeger Publishers, 1961.

Barke, James. *A History of Egypt From the Earliest Times to the End of the XVIII Dynasty.* London, A and C Black, Ltd, 1929.

Breasted, James Henry. *Ancient Records of Egypt: Historical Documents.* Chicago: University of Chicago Press, 1906.

———. *A History of Egypt.* New York, Scribner's and Sons, 1912.

Budge, E. A. Wallis. *Egyptian Magic.* New York: Dover Publications, 1971.

———. *The Gods of the Egyptians.* Vol II. New York: Dover Publications, 1969.

———. *Osiris and the Egyptian Resurrection.* New York: Dover Publications, 1973.

Casson, Lionel. *Ancient Egypt.* Alexandria, Va: Time-Life Books, 1978.

Crone, Patricia, and Michael Cook. *Hagarism: The Making of the Islamic World.* Cambridge: Cambridge University Press, 1940.

Cottrell, Leonard. *Egypt.* London: Nicholas Vane, 1965.

Edwards, I.E.S. *Pyramids of Egypt.* Baltimore: Penguin Books, 1961.

Emery, W. B. *Archaic Egypt.* Baltimore: Penguin Books, 1961.

Everyday Life in Bible Times. Washington, D.C.: National Geographic Society, 1967.

Fairservis, Jr., Walter A. *The Ancient Kingdoms of the Nile.* New York: New York American Library, 1962.

Frith, Francis. *Egypt and the Holy Land in Historic Photographs.* New York: Dover Publications, 1980.

Geraty, Lawrence T., and Larry G. Herr. *The Archaeology of Jordan and Other Studies.* Berrien Springs, Michigan: Andrews University Press, 1986.

Ginzberg, Louis. *Legends of the Bible.* Philadelphia: Jewish Publication Society, 1909.

Glueck, Nelson. *Rivers in the Desert.* New York: Grove Press, 1959.

Hawkes, Jacquetta, ed. *The World of the Past.* New York: Alfred A. Knopf, 1963.

Horn, Siegfried. *The Spade Confirms the Book.* Washington, D. C.: Review and Herald Pub. Assn., 1980.

Kramer, Samuel N. *The Sumerians: Their History, Culture, Character.* Chicago: University of Chicago Press, 1963.

Lichtheim, Miriam. *Ancient Egyptian Literature.* Vol. I. Berkley, Calif.: University of California Press, 1973.

Ludwig, Emil. *The Nile.* New York: Garden City Publishing Company, 1947.

Nevill, Peter. *Egyptian Art.* London: Spring House, Spring Place, 1962.

Mertz, Barbara. *Red Land, Black Land: Daily Life in Ancient Egypt.* New York: Dodd Mead and Company, 1978.

———. *Temples, Tombs and Heiroglyphs.* New York: Coward-McCann, Inc., 1964.

Moldenke, Harold N. *Plants of the Bible.* New York: The Ronald Press, 1952.

Morenz, Siegfried. *Egyptian Religion.* New York: Cornell University Press, 1973.

Pritchard, James B., ed. *Ancient Near Eastern Texts.* Princeton, N. J.: Princeton University Press, 1955.

———. *The Ancient Near East in Pictures Relating to the Old Testament.* Princeton, N. J: Princeton University Press, 1954.

Reader's Digest Atlas of the Bible. Pleasantville, N. Y.: Reader's Digest, 1981.

Sauneron, Serge. *The Priests of Ancient Egypt.* New York: Grove Press, 1980.

Shaw, Ian, and Paul Nicholson. *The Dictionary of Ancient Egypt.* New York: Harry N. Abrams, 1995.

Thompson, J. A. *The Bible and Archeology.* 3rd ed. Grand Rapids: William B. Eerdmans, 1982.

Wiseman, P. J. *Ancient Records and the Structure of Genesis.* New York: Thomas Nelson Publishers, 1985.

Wright, G. Ernest. *Biblical Archaeology.* Philadelphia: Westminster Press, 1957.